P9-AOO-427

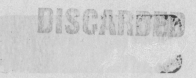
DATE DUE		

Maggie in the Morning

Maggie in the Morning

Elizabeth
Van Steenwyk

Eerdmans Books for Young Readers
Grand Rapids, Michigan • Cambridge, U.K.

© 2001 Elizabeth Van Steenwyk

Published 2001 by Eerdmans Books for Young Readers
an imprint of Wm. B. Eerdmans Publishing Co.
255 Jefferson Ave. S.E., Grand Rapids, Michigan 49503 /
P.O. Box 163, Cambridge CB3 9PU U.K.

Printed in the United States of America

01 02 03 04 05 06 07   7 6 5 4 3 2 1

Library of Congress Cataloging-in-Publication Data

Van Steenwyk, Elizabeth.
Maggie in the morning / written by Elizabeth Van Steenwyk. p.cm.
Summary: In 1941, while visiting relatives in Oquawka, Illinois,
eleven-year-old Maggie Calhoun is prodded by a spirited neighbor girl
to track down a family secret.
ISBN 0-8028-5222-X (cloth : alk. paper)
[1. Identity—Fiction. 2. Family life—Illinois—Fiction. 3. Secrets—Fiction.
4. Illinois—History—20th century—Fiction.] I. Title.

PZ7.V358 Mag 2001   [Fic] – dc21   2001023037

The display type was set in Bergell. The text type was set in Arrus.
Cover photograph © PhotoDisc. Cover design by Gayle Brown.

Dedicated to the memory of those saints
who brought so much joy to my early life,
especially my cousin, Phil.

One

Mom says I'm the luckiest girl in the world to have an Uncle Dick in my life and I say so too. Ever since he married Aunt Bess eight years ago, I visit them each summer. When my brother, Cooper, was old enough, he started coming, too. Uncle Dick says we're his best friends, and friends should always be there for one another through rain and shine and good times or bad. Good times are what we've always had at Uncle Dick's, until this summer when everything changed.

In some ways, things had changed even before the summer began. As the bus moved steadily down the highway to Uncle Dick's house in Oquawka, I thought about the changes. Endless fields of cornstalks shorter than Cooper's lanky six-year-old frame lined the highway like people at an

Odd Fellows' parade. Where would I be in September when those cornstalks were no longer green, but harvest brown?

"I'm homesick, Maggie," Cooper announced suddenly. He began to kick the bus seat in front of us with his scuffed-up Buster Browns. His shoelaces were untied as usual.

"But we just left."

"I know." He kicked harder.

"We like to go to Uncle Dick's, remember?"

"But this time we're going to stay longer, lots longer."

"So Mom can rest before the baby comes."

"Will Mom and Dad move to California without us?"

So that's what was bothering him. "Of course not, silly. After the baby is born, we'll all go together."

"But Dad said the baby might be sick." Cooper looked as if he might start crying any second.

"That's why Mom has to stay in bed. So the baby won't be born early and be so little that it'll be sick." I wasn't sure about what I was saying, but it must have satisfied Cooper.

Mom began to stay in bed a couple of weeks ago, right after school ended and I finished fifth grade. If that wasn't enough change for Cooper and me, Dad made his big announcement soon after. We were moving from Chicago to California as soon as Mom and the baby were okay because he was sure to find a job out there. The Depression was about over and jobs were available, thanks to the new defense industry, Dad said. Lots of people like him had lost their jobs and all their money — and even their houses — when they couldn't find work. I wasn't sure what a Depression was, but I knew I didn't like what it did.

"The way Hitler is stirring up things in Europe has got defense plants in this country handing out jobs right and left," Dad added. "And I aim to get one of them." Dad couldn't wait to make airplanes for the war that was coming.

A lot more was bothering me though. Lots more. When I hear Mom and Dad talk about the new baby and what it'll look like, they talk about themselves and Cooper, but never about me — Cooper's eyes, Mom's hair — never anything about my nose or my hair or my eyes. Don't they figure I've noticed that? It's something that really makes me wonder. Could I look like some relative that no one wants to talk about because she's locked up in a loony bin somewhere?

That thought wandered through my head again as the bus passed farms that looked as patched and faded as some of Grandanna's old quilts. Times had been hard on everybody, and maybe there still wasn't much call for Uncle Dick to move houses. That's his line of work. It might look hard to some people, but not to Uncle Dick. He moves real houses from one place to another the way most people move them from Park Place to Boardwalk in a game of Monopoly. Once I heard him say he'd probably moved half of Oquawka by this time. But he was only joking. I could see all of it now as we pulled into the bus station.

Oquawka is so small it hardly makes a dent in the highway. It's nestled in a curve of the Mississippi River, and if you can spell that you can spell anything. At least that's what Uncle Dick says. And most times, he's right.

He was waiting at the depot, and his hug smelled like pine tar soap and wood shavings. His bristly face scratched mine until it tingled.

"Look at you two," he said, sizing us up. "You've grown like hollyhocks since you were here last."

"I'm going to start school in September," Cooper said. "I'll be the tallest one in first grade."

"Never too tall to hug." Uncle Dick squeezed him again.

I looked around. "Where's Aunt Bess?" Normally she was flitting around, chattering like a tufted jay.

Uncle Dick ran a hand over his patent-leather-shiny-black hair. "Cooking up a fine supper for us." He grabbed our suitcases and headed for the parking lot. "Before supper though, I have to see a man about a house."

As we climbed into Uncle Dick's old truck, I noticed that at least nothing had changed inside it. It was still as messy as ever. On the floor an old baloney sandwich had curled and browned to cardboard stiffness, paintbrushes bristled on the seat waiting to attack our legs, and three-penny nails rolled back and forth on the dashboard as Uncle Dick drove out of the parking lot.

We headed for the country, which doesn't take long in a town the size of Oquawka. A little while later we turned off the highway onto an old dirt road that looked as if it had been forgotten on the county map.

Soon we came to the house that was going to be moved. It had already been jacked up and away from its foundation. Now it was sitting on the jacks and a lot of air.

"Are you ready to move, house?" Uncle Dick shouted as he jumped out. He likes to talk to his houses.

We waited inside the truck while Uncle Dick walked over and spoke to a man and woman who were standing by the porch. She was wearing a dark hat with a wide brim that shadowed her face. Uncle Dick took a map from his pocket and they all pointed at it while they talked. Then Uncle Dick shook hands with the man, patted the lady on the shoulder, and hurried back to us.

He rolled up the sleeves of his plaid shirt, then leaned against the steering wheel as he stared at the house. "Gonna be a tough one, but I can do it," he said.

He started the motor. "I'm going to take the route I'll use when I move the house," he said. "Don't think you've been this way before, and it takes longer to get home, I know. But I can't have any surprises at the last second." He wheeled around and we headed up another road.

"Why do those folks back there want to move?" Cooper asked.

"They lost their land to the bank, but the banker said they could have the house if they moved it. So that's what they're going to do."

"Is the house empty?" Cooper asked again.

"No." Suddenly Uncle Dick's voice was soft. "It's full of memories."

Suddenly so was I, memories that didn't quite focus. A few of them began to flash through my brain. If only one or two of the images would become clearer, maybe I could see what they were and what they meant.

The truck picked up speed before we raced by a sign on a farmhouse fence. "Ponies For Sale," I read aloud.

"Ponies?" Cooper sat up straight. "Can we go back and look at them, Uncle Dick?"

"I didn't see any ponies," Uncle Dick said. He didn't slow down either.

"But the sign." I pointed backwards. "It said 'Ponies For

Sale.'"

"Are you sure?" Uncle Dick asked.

"Absolutely, for a fact."

"I'll bet you an ice cream cone the sign didn't say that."
Then Uncle Dick grinned. He really loves teasing.

"Go on, Maggie," Cooper said. "Bet him." He knew there
was ice cream in it for him, too.

"It's a double-decker bet," I answered, already tasting my
prize.

Uncle Dick stopped the truck, but there was no place to
turn around. So he backed up all the way to the farmhouse
where the sign was tacked to a fence. I read it and watched
my ice cream cone melt in my mind.

"I see it, Uncle Dick," I said. "Peonies For Sale."

"What are peonies?" Cooper asked.

"Flowers," I answered. "P-E-O-N-I-E-S. I just learned
how to spell it."

"Then I think that calls for a celebration." Uncle Dick
shifted the truck into forward. "Anyone who can spell
peonies ought to be rewarded with a double-decker ice cream
cone."

"I'll know how to spell it by the time we get there,"
Cooper said.

And then I was looking at a suddenly-focused and

brightly-shining picture inside my head. A lady used to come and see me when I was very small, and she always wore a big black hat with a blue flower on it like the lady's on the porch. She brought me peppermints and paper dolls, until one day she suddenly stopped coming. After a while she seemed like a dream or as though she'd never been, because no one told me who she was or where she'd gone. Now her face is like a wrinkled shadow in my mind, but the big black hat with blue flower on it is as brightly-focused as if it were here in Uncle Dick's truck beside me.

I wonder if Uncle Dick knows who she is.

Two

Aunt Bess was in the backyard pulling weeds when we arrived after a stop at Highlander's for ice cream. She wore a faded straw hat she'd owned ever since I could remember. Its floppy brim had enough waves on it to make a fly seasick. Now she ran across the lawn towards us, holding up a basket stuffed full of greenery.

She gave enormous hugs for a tiny lady. Then she held up her basket of weeds again. "Just look," she said, her dark eyes dancing. "Lamb's-quarters, dandelion leaves, purslane, curly dock, and wild onion. We'll have a feast tonight."

"Feast?" Cooper asked, looking up at me and pulling on my skirt at the same time.

"Aunt Bess's salad, how could you forget?" I said,

grabbing his hand and pulling him along with us.

"Easy," he muttered, dragging his Buster Browns on the grass.

We followed Aunt Bess through the kitchen and into the dining room. While the others headed for the sunroom where Cooper and I always slept, I stopped and leaned against the huge stone fireplace that occupied most of one wall. Now it was cool to the touch, but on every Thanksgiving Day I could remember, Uncle Dick and the fireplace roared together with warmth and good cheer, presiding over a table that looked ready to collapse with the weight of the food. Gathered around were aunts, uncles, cousins, and of course, Grandanna. It was a feast for body and heart around that table on that day.

I followed Aunt Bess and Cooper into the sunroom as Uncle Dick's voice filled the house even now. He'd gone upstairs to the unfinished attic he called his office and was talking on the telephone about forms and permits. He must be planning to move that house soon.

Cooper and I unpacked while Aunt Bess put finishing touches on our supper. When she called, we didn't waste a second getting to the table. Uncle Dick clattered down the stairs, still in his heavy work boots, and came into the kitchen right behind us. Cooper sighed when he spotted the weeds in the salad bowl, but he didn't complain one bit after Aunt Bess brought our favorite spaghetti soufflé to the table. Its cheesy top looked ready to float up to the ceiling.

We ate for a while in dedicated silence. "That sure was good," Cooper finally said. He wiped his mouth on his shirtsleeve, ignoring his napkin. "Even the weeds."

Aunt Bess looked pleased. "One thing about them," she said. "I'll have a brand new crop tomorrow."

"I never thought of that." Cooper's face took on the look it got just before Mom gave him his cod liver oil.

"How's your mama feeling?" Aunt Bess asked. "I hope that talk about moving to California hasn't come at a bad time for Edie."

I didn't know how to answer. But that didn't stop Cooper.

"Mom doesn't want to go," he stated, as if he had the last word on it.

"Cooper, you don't know that," I began.

"Just what I thought." Aunt Bess began to fan her face with a corner of her apron. "Don't know why your folks can't come home to Oquawka and your papa could get a job at the feed store. You could fix it for him, Dick."

"Now Bess, we've got no right to interfere. Fred wants to go to California. He'll find a job without any help from anybody."

"And all this talk about defense plants making planes and bombs can't be good for the children to hear. There's no call to be scaring Cooper and Maggie." Aunt Bess wasn't going to leave it alone.

"Put all of that out of your minds, kids," Uncle Dick rushed his words. "We got to make plans to have a little fun while you're here."

"What have you got in mind, Dick?" Aunt Bess carried some dishes to the sink.

"Well, the carnival is in town," he said, "and the Methodists are having an ice cream social to raise money to buy new hymn books."

Aunt Bess whirled around, her dark, curly hair trembling like a blackberry bush in a hailstorm. "Seems to me, Dick Slocum, you're offering a choice to those children between sin and salvation." She reached to a shelf above the stove, snapped on the radio, and the Jack Benny Show flooded the room. The conversation had ended.

Uncle Dick's face clouded over with concern as he hurried over to Aunt Bess and gave her a big hug. "How about getting everybody together for a fish fry down on the island next Sunday?" he shouted over Jack Benny.

Aunt Bess fanned her face with a dishcloth. "Then

somebody's got to do some serious fishing beforehand," she said.

"That's Grandanna's job," I said. I took the dishcloth from Aunt Bess and began to wipe.

"Maggie, why don't you and Cooper run over to Grandanna's to see if she's interested?" Uncle Dick turned so that only I could see him as he gave me a big wink. "We'll catch up with you in a few minutes."

He wanted us out of there, and I obliged. "Come on, Cooper, let's go."

"But I want to listen to Jack Benny and Rochester. They're funny."

"Next week," I said, grabbing his arm.

Two blocks and ten minutes later, we walked up the steps to Grandanna's porch and opened the screen door. "Hello," I called.

We listened and waited in her parlor, still warm from the twilight sun. Dust motes floated along on an unfelt shift of air.

"Turn on the light," Cooper whispered. "It's practically dark." He stepped close to me and I put my arm around his skinny shoulders. Then I snapped on the ceiling light and we stood blinking in its glare.

"Goodness sake, you liked to scare me to death." Aunt

Lolly, Mom's next to oldest sister, stood in the kitchen doorway. She wore a hat that looked like one of Grandanna's pan lids.

"Sorry, Aunt Lolly, I didn't know you were here," I said. "Don't really need these lights yet, not when there's still light outside." She glanced past us to the open doorway.

"But it's almost . . . " Cooper started to say, but I gave his shoulders a little pinch.

In the family people say that Aunt Lolly likes to squeeze every penny until she's got her dollar's worth.

"Why are you wearing your hat in the house?" Cooper asked.

"Just got home from a funeral," Aunt Lolly replied.

"Who died?" Cooper couldn't keep his mouth shut.

"A nice old man." Aunt Lolly's mouth set itself in a straight pencil line across her face.

"What was his name?" Cooper persisted.

"Cooper," I sounded a warning note. Probably he didn't know Aunt Lolly went to funerals a lot. It was kind of her hobby. She said it was a good way to meet folks and they always had good eats afterwards.

She turned out the parlor light, so I walked into the kitchen and turned on the kitchen lamp. Cooper and Aunt Lolly followed me.

"Where's Grandanna?" I asked. "Still working?"

"No, she's in bed, sound asleep. She about wore herself out today, weaving the last of the rugs for the craft show at the fair. And I'm on my way to Roy's store to help him make doughnuts." Roy Luvall and Aunt Lolly had been keeping company since Uncle Art fell in a snowdrift and died six years ago.

"Can I come with you?" Cooper asked. "I love doughnuts."

"Some other time." Aunt Lolly took off her hat and ran a hand through her hair. "Besides, you must be tired from your long bus ride today."

"Not when you're as old as I am," he answered. "Do you know how far it is to California? It's a lot longer than . . . "

"Come on, Cooper, Aunt Lolly's right. We need to go to bed early tonight too."

We started back to Aunt Bess and Uncle Dick's house. Somehow I got the feeling that we were underfoot at both houses. Aunt Lolly had been waiting for Roy to pop the question for so long, she probably didn't want to let any opportunity slip by.

Lightning bugs blinked in our path as we walked slowly towards the corner.

"Maggie." Cooper put his hand in mine. "Is she really

our aunt?"

"Who, Aunt Lolly?"

"Yes."

"Do you mean is she really Mom's sister?" I asked. "Of course. Why do you ask?"

"She's so different. Not real friendly like Mom or Aunt Bess."

"Maybe she's having an unfriendly day." But it was true. Aunt Lolly never smiled.

We had walked nearly to the corner before we heard the music. Finally, something cheerful. "Come on, Cooper. Frank Cunningham's band is tuning up."

When Frank and Mom went to high school together, Mom said he won every music award in the district. She tried to get him to go on Major Bowes Amateur Hour to be discovered, but he had to go to work instead. Now he was chief inspector at the blue jeans factory, but his dance band played at the Elks Lodge every Saturday night.

We tiptoed up the cement steps to Frank's porch and peeked inside the open window. Frank sat at the piano playing without sheet music. Mac Butler was playing the trombone and Slim Jupiter kept time on the drums. I'd never seen the guys on the saxophone or guitar. They must be new since last summer. Now they played old time dance tunes one after the other while my feet tried to keep up. So did Cooper's. Suddenly Aunt Bess and Uncle Dick appeared at the bottom of the steps.

"Thought we'd find you here," Uncle Dick whispered. "We know how much you like Frank's music."

Then he gathered Aunt Bess into his arms, and they began to dance on the cement driveway, dipping and swaying as if they didn't have a care in the world.

A few minutes later, as we walked home, I glanced up at Uncle Dick's face. We were under the streetlight, and I could see him clearly. A frown line, shaped like a feeder creek to the river, meandered across his forehead. Was he worried about moving the house, or about something concerning Aunt Bess? Maybe something had happened since we were here for Christmas, or maybe I was just noticing things more now that I was older. Either way, I didn't like the feeling.

Three

Uncle Dick was already gone when I got up the next morning so I couldn't ask him questions that were waiting in my mind. Soon, though, I needed to talk to him. That's one of the great things about Uncle Dick. He always makes room for kids like me and Cooper when we need to talk to a grownup. I don't know where he learned how to do that either. He doesn't have any kids of his own so he hasn't had any practice.

I walked out to the kitchen for breakfast. While Aunt Bess flipped skinny pancakes, then rolled them around strawberries and broke honeycomb over the top, she explained that Uncle Dick wanted to be first in line at the city hall to get the papers he needed.

"Papers? What kind of papers?" Cooper asked as he shoveled pancakes into his mouth.

"Papers to move that farmhouse." Aunt Bess sat down with a cup of coffee in front of her. "It takes a lot of government interference to move one little old house."

She stared out the window for a second. Then she said, "I wonder who that little girl is out there."

Cooper and I looked. As we watched, the girl quickly cut through some bushes at the back and disappeared from view. I'd barely caught a glimpse of her.

I turned to look at Aunt Bess again while she sipped her coffee. She didn't seem as wound up this morning as she had last night. Maybe she was getting used to us again. After all, she'd never had kids either. She and Uncle Dick were pretty old when they got married and probably didn't want to be bothered with babies.

"I hope we're not too much trouble," I began. "Maybe Mom will have the baby early, and we can go home sooner."

"What are you talking about, dear Maggie?" Aunt Bess reached over and gave my arm a pat. "We want you to stay as long as you like. Longer than last year."

"But we have to go to California," Cooper said, wiping his mouth on his pajama sleeve. "Dad has to make planes and things."

"Thanks, Aunt Bess," I said. "I thought, well, last night . . . "

"Never mind last night," she said. "I just let my nerves get to me."

"I think I smell Ovaltine cooking," Cooper said.

Aunt Bess nearly leaped out of her chair. "You smell it burning, more's the like."

She snatched a pan from the stove and stared into it. "I'll make some more."

"Will you let me have the label as soon as the jar is empty?" Cooper asked. "I want to get a Little Orphan Annie secret decoder ring just like Maggie's."

While he drank two cups of Ovaltine, we decided to go see Grandanna first thing this morning so we could plan the fish fry for next Sunday. Nobody else could chum the fish onto the line the way she could.

Aunt Bess was ironing Uncle Dick's underwear and listening to "Our Gal Sunday" when we left for Grandanna's. We had just passed Frank Cunningham's house when I knew we were being followed, or at least watched. I'd sensed it ever since we turned the corner. A couple of times I turned but saw no one. But she was there, I knew it.

"What's wrong?" Cooper asked.

"Nothing." It couldn't be anyone I knew.

"There's somebody in the bushes by Frank's front porch," Cooper said, turning around.

"Is it that girl we saw in Aunt Bess's backyard?"

"Maybe. She's got whitish hair, kind of."

"You mean blonde?" It might have been Marjorie Watson acting dumb, but I hadn't seen her since last summer, so I wasn't sure.

"What's blonde?"

"You know, like Shirley Temple. She's kind of blonde. Or Carole Lombard, the actress that dad likes."

"I don't think that's Carole Lombard back there in the bushes."

"Oh, Cooper, never mind."

We turned in at Grandanna's and banged the screen door as we went inside. Her weaving loom thumped steadily in the basement.

"Sounds like Grandanna's making another rug," Cooper said, dashing for the basement door and opening it.

We stopped on the first step, sniffed like a couple of puppy dogs, and yelled "root beer" at the same time. Then we clattered down the steps and raced to Grandanna seated on a bench in front of her loom.

"Grandanna, you made root beer again!" Cooper shouted, reaching up to hug her. After it blew up all over the basement last year, she told everyone she wouldn't make it anymore.

"A girl's got a right to change her mind," she said. She put down her spindle and hopped off the bench to hug me too. Smaller than Aunt Bess, she could hug just as hard.

For a moment she just looked at me. "My, how you've growed," she said softly. "You're built different than the rest of the women in the family, that's for sure. So tall and spare."

I suddenly realized that I was eye level with her, and we just stood there taking in the newness of it.

She took my measure some more then started in on herself, beginning first with her flat, black shoes laced loosely over crooked, bumpy feet, then at her faded dress under a flour-sack apron pulled over her sagging body. Finally, she straightened up a bit and felt her hair, thick, red waves of it held captive in a braided bun that looked as if it had been sprinkled with salt.

She sighed. "I wasn't always this old," she said before she led the way upstairs.

Cooper sat down at the cloth-covered kitchen table and began to play Sunday School with all the medicine bottles gathered on a plate in the center. It was a game I'd invented and taught him. First, he arranged the tallest bottle in the middle of a row, then smaller ones on either side down to the squat Vicks Vapor Rub bottles on each end, just like the kids were arranged on the platform in Sunday School programs.

Then Cooper put the game into action. He moved the tallest kid, the Fletcher's Castoria bottle, one step forward and began to sing his solo, "Jesus Wants Me for a Sunbeam." Cooper could really carry a tune for a six-year-old.

A sudden movement outside the window above the sink caught my attention. It was that girl from Aunt Bess's backyard. Grandanna saw her too and raced for the screen door.

"Ida Mae George, quit trampin' around on my flowers and come in here this minute." A second later a girl about my age stepped into the kitchen. Her hair looked like a pile of dusty-white cotton candy.

"You remember Mrs. Dean who lives two doors down?" Grandanna asked me. Without waiting for an answer, she went on. "This here's her granddaughter visiting from Peoria. I told her you and Cooper were coming."

"You've got a wart on your hand," Ida Mae said, looking at me with pale eyes ringed by lashes that looked as if they were made of cobwebs. "Why don't you get rid of that ugly thing?"

I stepped back, instantly disliking her. The only thing I

hated more than my wart was someone who noticed it and then talked about it.

"Do you want to play Sunday School?" Cooper asked.

"Hell, no." Ida Mae turned her no-color stare on him.

"Listen here, young lady, you don't talk like that in my house." Grandanna's eyes started to blaze before she took a breath. "Now, why don't we settle ourselves and have a glass of root beer?"

"I'll help you." Cooper skirted around Ida Mae and raced after Grandanna down the basement stairs.

"My grandma can get rid of your wart," Ida Mae said. She was bound to keep talking about it. "All she has to do is rub a chicken gizzard on it by the light of the moon. The bigger the better."

"The bigger the wart?"

"No, the bigger the moon."

"I'm not interested."

"What's the matter? Are you skeered?"

"Of course not. Mom says the doctor's got to do it."

"Don't need no doctor when my grandma's around. She's got the gift. She knows everything. She knows all about you."

My heart gave an extra little thump. Was this strange girl talking through her hat, or did her grandma know something special about me?

"Well, maybe I'll think about the chicken gizzard thing." I hoped I looked as if I was thinking really hard. "But where am I going to get one?"

"Go to Roy's store when he brings in a fresh bunch of chickens. He butchers out back, you know. A lot of people don't like to eat the gizzards, so he throws them out for the dogs."

"I felt shuddery inside and began to taste breakfast all over again. "Maybe," I began. "Maybe."

"Oh, don't worry about it. I'll go over there and get a gizzard for you. If you're gonna be my friend, you gotta get rid of that wart first."

I looked at her, wondering where she got the idea that I wanted to be her friend. Maybe in a million years.

Grandanna came upstairs with a pitcher of root beer. Cooper was right behind her, already wearing a foamy root beer mustache. He must have been dipping in the crock.

Ida Mae drank her glass of root beer without taking a breath while Cooper watched, open-mouthed. I knew he was going to try it and he did right then, making a funny gulping sound.

"Maggie," Grandanna said. "There's some clothes up in the attic that I want to get ready for your mama's new baby.

Would you mind going up to fetch them for me? My knees are about wore out today."

"Sure, Grandanna. Were they Mom's clothes when she was a baby?"

"No, honey, they were yours. There's two pink boxes full of things I know she'll want to have, especially if she has a little girl."

"Why do you have my baby clothes? Why doesn't Mom have them like she has Cooper's?"

Grandanna looked outside before answering as if she might find a reason hanging from the cherry tree. "Don't rightly know. They just got in my attic, by mistake maybe, and then forgot until now. Of course, when Cooper was born, your daddy wouldn't hear of him wearing pink."

A strange noise rolled up out of Cooper. When I looked at him, he was hanging on to his stomach and rocking back and forth. Uh, oh! All that Ovaltine he drank earlier must be resenting the root beer.

"Cooper, what's the matter?" I looked at him closely. "Do you want to throw up?"

"No, but I think I'm going to." He ran for the bathroom with Grandanna right behind him.

"Bet my grandma knows why your baby clothes got left," Ida Mae whispered. Then she grinned, and I hated her more than ever.

Later when Grandanna came back she'd forgotten about the baby clothes, but I hadn't.

Four

Even before I opened my eyes the next morning, I knew it was raining tiddlywinks and dominoes. Rain pounded on all nine windows in the sunroom, but it seemed to be making a ringing sound instead of a raining sound. Then I knew the ringing came from something else. It was the telephone in the kitchen.

I sat up, wide-awake now. The dull glow of a rainy dawn told me it was way too early for any good news to come from the telephone. Only bad news happened this early. Maybe something had happened to Mom or the baby yet to be born. Maybe the baby had tried to come too soon.

I ran from the sunroom, trying not to wake up Cooper, but I shouldn't have worried. He could sleep through an air raid just like the ones the newspapers said they were having in London right now.

The kitchen was bright with light as I rounded the corner of the dining room, and I could hear Uncle Dick's low rumble. He and Aunt Bess had a telephone upstairs in their bedroom, but he must have been up already. Yes, I could tell from the coffeepot perking away on the stove.

"Just a minute," he was saying. "Here she is." He held out the telephone receiver to me.

"Mom? Is she all right?" Suddenly my feet were freezing on the linoleum floor. "Hello." I was so scared.

"Morning, Maggie. You took your own sweet time coming to the telephone."

Oh, no. I gave a big, deep sigh, so relieved I couldn't find my voice. Then I began to simmer and boil, just like the coffee.

"Ida Mae, what are you calling so early for?"

"I wanted to get a head start on my vacation," she said. "I got lots of things planned for us to do."

"Don't you know what time it is?" I yelled.

"Of course I do," she yelled back. "We got a clock over here same as everybody else. Can you come over and play or not? And when are you coming over to get your wart taken off? And that other thing you want to talk about to my grandma."

"You mean you want me to come over right now?"

"What did you think I meant? Tomorrow or next week? You got a better time in mind?"

"I haven't had breakfast yet." I was stalling, trying to think of something to say to get rid of her. Besides, I wish she hadn't said that stuff about me wanting to talk to her grandma. Maybe Uncle Dick had heard her.

Now he was motioning by the table, pointing to the oatmeal bowls and toast he'd put on it.

"My uncle says I have to eat right now."

"How about after?"

I looked at Uncle Dick for help. He made big motions with his hands as if he were driving a car and then waving goodbye.

"Then I have to go someplace."

"Where? Can I go too?"

"Gee whiz, Ida Mae, you're supposed to let me do the asking."

There was a long pause before she said, "Not many kids do."

"I'll call you back after breakfast," I said, and hung up before she could ask more questions.

Aunt Bess walked in, looking like a sleepy little girl

without her glasses. "What in tarnation is going on?" she asked.

Uncle Dick poured two cups of coffee and brought them to the table. "Maggie got a phone call."

Aunt Bess sat down, her seersucker kimono dragging on the floor. "About your mama?"

"No." Then I sat down beside her to explain about Ida Mae. "I wish she'd leave me alone," I finished. "She's getting to be a pest."

Uncle Dick spread strawberry jam on a slab of whole-wheat toast. "Tell you what," he began. "I'm going out to the house this afternoon, rain or shine, and figured to invite you to go along, Maggie. I got to see what this weather is doing to the footing I put down alongside the foundation of the house."

I knew what he was going to say and tried to get ready for it.

"Why don't you invite that girl to go along?" A bit of jam spilled on his plaid shirt but you could barely see it.

"Why don't you come along, Aunt Bess?" I suggested. Maybe she could tame Ida Mae.

"I need to stay here," she said. "The cherries I picked yesterday got to be canned this morning."

"We can handle Ida Mae," Uncle Dick said. "Besides, I

think she's just lonesome. Maybe all she needs is a little cheering up and we got extra of that to go around."

Cooper stumbled into the kitchen, rubbing his eyes with both fists. "Is it still yesterday, or is it tomorrow?" he asked.

"It's tomorrow," I told him.

"Good, then I can eat breakfast." He climbed on a chair and waited as Uncle Dick ladled oatmeal into his bowl.

"Ida Mae's going with us out to see the house to be moved," I began.

"Then I'm not," Cooper said quickly. "She's too spooky for me."

Aunt Bess turned on the radio as I left the room to get dressed. The announcer was saying something about Germany continuing its offensive against Russia. I wasn't sure what that news meant for our country, but it sounded plenty serious. Maybe I'd get a chance to ask Uncle Dick about the war on the ride out to the moving job.

It would have been easier to ask President Roosevelt. Ida Mae was so excited about being asked to go along to the country that she never stopped talking. Even Uncle Dick was amazed, and he doesn't amaze too easy.

A while later Uncle Dick stopped the pickup on the road in front of the house, then told us to wait while he inspected the foundation work. The rain was coming down in whiskery sprinkles now, instead of the gully wumper it had been. The air grew hot and sticky inside the truck.

"Never knew a person who moved houses before," Ida Mae said, watching Uncle Dick slog through the mud towards the house. "He must be pretty strong."

"He doesn't pick them up all by himself." I sounded pretty snotty. "He's got a lot of equipment, but he can't get it in here until it dries out and . . . "

"I know that." She about bit my head off. "Think I was born yestereday?"

"Ida Mae, why are you always so crabby?"

"This ain't crabby. You ought to hear my ma's new boyfriend. He's always yellin' after me."

How many boyfriends did her ma have anyways?

We both began to scratch at the same time.

"Skeeters are gonna eat us alive," she said.

"As soon as Uncle Dick comes back, maybe he'll light up a cigar and drive the bugs away with the smoke."

"Where's he keep his smokes?" Ida Mae looked at me intently with her pale blue eyes. "Bet they're in here."

Without waiting, she opened the glove compartment to reveal several stogies. Ida Mae grabbed two, both with cellophane paper covering them and "It's a Boy" stamped across one side.

"One for you and one for me," she said, bringing out a box of kitchen matches as well.

"I'm not gonna smoke that thing," I said. "It stinks."

"Then keep on scratchin'," she said, ripping paper from the cigar. It took her a few tries, but she finally got it going and began to sputter and cough at the same time.

"You'd try it too if you weren't such a scaredy cat." Tears welled in her eyes.

"I'm not a scaredy cat," I snapped back at her. "You're all the time calling names. Cut it out."

"Prove it, then." She coughed several times before she could go on. "Light up."

In a minute I was puffing away, mad as a banty rooster because I was doing what she wanted me to do. Wouldn't I just love to get back at her.

"Did you find out anything about . . . you know . . . anything?" She disappeared into a cloud of smoke.

"What do you mean, anything?" The inside of the truck began to spin now even before I took another puff.

"You know, what my grandma knows about you and what you wanna find out."

She'd been asking questions already. "Stay out of it, Ida Mae. Mind your own beeswax."

"You're just a scaredy cat in that department too. You're

the afraidest person I ever knew. If I was you, I'd be askin' questions, gettin' answers . . . "

"Well, you're not me. What do you know about anything?"

"You're not scratchin' any more, are you?"

Maybe I wasn't scratching, but I sure was spinning and vowed never to light up again. Uncle Dick came back in a few minutes and smiled as he looked at us. "Think you girls could stand a little air and some exercise."

We drove down the road to a place where the woods collide with the riverbank. Tall oaks and black walnut trees grew in a thick tangle as if to protect mossbanks and lacy ferns beneath them.

"What are we doing here?" Ida Mae asked, rubbing her eyes.

Uncle Dick took off his light jacket. "Lookin' for supper," he said. Then he began to pull back ferns and undergrowth.

"Mushrooms!" I shouted.

"Mind which ones you pick," Uncle Dick reminded me, finding one that looked like a sponge on a stalk.

Ida Mae began to look too. "Is this a good one?" she asked.

"Nope, throw it back." Uncle Dick gently placed another mushroom in the center of his jacket. "That one's poisonous."

"Poisonous?" Ida Mae stared at him in disbelief.

"You die a terrible, lingering death if you eat a bad one." I couldn't help it. I just had to say it.

"No kidding?" she asked.

"No kidding," I repeated.

When the jacket was full we drove slowly home as the clouds parted to give the sun a place to shine through.

We walked into the kitchen to find Aunt Bess finishing the last of the cherries. Bright cheery jars lined one counter and a freshly baked pie sat alongside. A rich, sugary sauce dripped from its crust like a dark red lava flow.

"We don't have much pie at our house," Ida Mae said. "That one sure looks good."

"Why don't you stay to supper?" Aunt Bess asked. "Call your grandma and ask if you can."

"Don't need to." A broad smile took root on Ida Mae's face. "I pretty much come and go as I like."

Cooper stood at the sink, husking corn ears, but the rest of us pitched in to gently wash the fragile mushrooms, then soak them in salt water until Aunt Bess was ready. Now she sliced them lengthwise, then dipped them in an egg wash and cracker crumbs before she fried them in butter.

A few minutes later supper was on the table, a bowl of

freshly boiled sweet corn and a stack of lighter-than-air mushrooms, crisp but still tasting of their musky, earthly beginnings.

Then I noticed Ida Mae. She wasn't eating but was watching us with panic in her face. I couldn't stop myself. If I didn't say it, I'd burst.

"What's the matter, Ida Mae?" I asked ever so sweetly. "You afraid to eat the mushrooms? You're not a scaredy cat, are you?"

Aunt Bess frowned at me as she explained that Uncle Dick had been picking these mushrooms since he was a pup so he knew a thing or two about which ones were which.

Slowly, Ida Mae began to nibble on the food although she never took her eyes off me for the rest of the meal.

I didn't care. My eyes were on the pie, although it would have to wait until I had room for it.

But it looked like Ida Mae had already made room for herself at this table. I began to wonder if she'd ever go home.

Five

Ida Mae left me alone for a couple of days after I made fun of her because she was scared to eat the mushrooms. Funny thing, though. I kind of missed her the same way you miss a bee sting after it stops stinging. You don't know what to complain about any more.

On Friday afternoon Uncle Dick and Cooper went fishing to help Grandanna with the fish fry on Sunday. Uncle Dick was going to try for some more catfish and striped bass since they were the best for frying. Aunt Bess and I stayed home because she decided to sew a new dress for me. She had just laid out the pattern over some green cotton print when the telephone rang. Mom and the baby-to-be were always on my mind so my heart pounded a bit harder as I waited for Aunt Bess to take pins out of her mouth to answer.

"I declare," Aunt Bess said, after she listened for a minute. "Just calm down, Grandanna, I'll be right over."

She turned to me. "I may need your help, Maggie. Come on."

"What's the matter?" I ran out the door and down the porch steps after her.

"It's Lolly." Aunt Bess's brown oxfords sounded like clicker beetles as she marched along on the brick sidewalk. "She came home from Roy's and went up to the attic to stay forever. Least that's what she told Grandanna." Aunt Bess paused at the corner to catch her breath. "And she acted like she meant it too, because she pulled the attic ladder up after her."

"She'll come down when she has to go to the toilet." I was practical in all things. "She probably had a fight with Roy. She's been waiting for him for a long time, and she's not getting any younger."

Aunt Bess attacked the next block on a trot. "Now, Maggie, that's not a nice thing to say although it does happen to be true. Come to think of it, she waited a long time for Art to pop the question too."

"Maybe she just picks the slow ones."

We turned the corner and walked by Ida Mae's grandma's house, but there wasn't a sign of either one of them.

Now we turned in at Grandanna's. "I wish . . . ," Aunt Bess started to say.

"What?"

"I wish me and my sisters weren't so complicated." Her voice quivered a little.

Maybe this was more serious than I thought. What did she mean that she and her sisters were so complicated? Anybody could tell that Aunt Lolly had a different streak to her. But Mom? And Aunt Bess? They seemed normal, at least for grown-ups. Mom was the youngest sister and got married early. Aunt Bess was the oldest and worked for years at this real important job in the courthouse. She met Uncle Dick there when he came in to get his house moving papers straightened out. Aunt Lolly was the middle sister and spent most of her life waiting for something to happen. As near as I could tell, she was the only one who was complicated.

We hurried inside and found Grandanna in the kitchen staring up at the ceiling.

"She hasn't made a sound since she went up there," Grandanna said. "S'pose Lolly's fainted in all this heat? She's pretty delicate."

"She's as strong as a flag pole." Aunt Bess gave Grandanna a hug.

Grandanna shrugged Aunt Bess away from her and turned her fierce gaze on me. "Maggie, how are you at climbing ladders?"

So that was it. They were going to send me up to get Aunt Lolly. At the same time though, I could use the opportunity to look around up there. "I can manage."

"There's a ladder out in the garden shed. You girls run along and fetch it."

Aunt Bess and I hurried outside and met Ida Mae just leaping over the hedge separating Grandanna's yard from her neighbor's.

"Maggie, you went right by our house and didn't look or nothin'. Did somebody die?"

"No, but it's kind of an emergency." I opened the door to the shed.

"I'm good at that." Ida Mae's face brightened as if someone had just volunteered to wipe the dishes when it was her turn.

She followed us into the shed, grabbed one end of the ladder, and helped us carry it into the house.

"Run along, Ida Mae," Grandanna said. "We got family business here."

Her tone left no doubt. Ida Mae backed out, slamming the screen door behind her. Quickly we set up the ladder under the trap door opening to the attic.

"Now just go up there and pound on the door," Aunt Bess said.

I climbed the ladder and, when I could reach, began to pound on the trap door. Then I shoved with both hands.

"I think she's pushed something across the door," I said, looking down at Aunt Bess and Grandanna. "It won't budge. Maybe she doesn't want company right now."

"She don't know what she wants or she wouldn't be up there in the first place." Grandanna sounded snappish. "Chum her into a little conversation, Maggie."

"Aunt Lolly," I called in my syrupy-best voice. "Can I come up there with you?"

"No." Her voice sounded muffled on the other side of the door. "Go away."

I looked down. "See? What did I tell you?"

"I think you're right," Aunt Bess said. "Let's give her some room."

But Grandanna wasn't ready to give up. "What about the outside window? Think you can reach it, Maggie?"

My stomach lurched. Climbing a ladder inside the house was one thing, but teetering on one outdoors and having to crawl in a window I could just barely reach was another kettle of fish.

"I vote we wait until Uncle Dick gets home," I began.

"No," Grandanna said. "She'll just sit up there and get moody."

"She was born that way," I muttered, climbing down.

But Grandanna hadn't heard me. She was already outside, staring up at the attic window. Ida Mae stood watching in the shade of the cherry tree, alive now with the sound of bees drunk on fruit gone bad.

As Aunt Bess and I positioned the ladder, I could see there was a lot of house between the end of the ladder and the beginning of the attic window.

"I don't know if I can make it," I began.

"You want someone to git in that window?" Ida Mae sprang to life. "I'll do it if Maggie's scared to, Grandanna."

She's my grandma, I wanted to shout. But I didn't. "I didn't say I was scared to," I said. But Ida Mae knew what I meant.

I took possession of the ladder and began to climb. At the top I could just manage to reach the window. It seemed stuck at first, then with a final push, it opened and I got a face full of dust and spider webs for my trouble. Without daring to look down at the ground even once, I climbed in and fell in a heap on the dirty attic floor.

"I told you not to come up here."

Aunt Lolly's voice came from a dark corner where she sat on an old footstool. She must be melting over there, it was hotter than Hades right here by the window.

"Grandanna's worried sick about you, Aunt Lolly." I stood up and walked toward her. Then I saw them sitting side by side in the corner. The baby boxes that Grandanna had talked about the other night sat there in a kind of pink glow, beckoning me to discover their secrets. My baby clothes. Would I find anything tucked in the boxes with them? Grownups keep the strangest stuff, but sometimes it's telling. Back in the olden days, people kept things that told about their civilization way back then. Maybe those pink boxes will be written up in history books one day. It could happen.

Now, though, I had to keep my mind on Aunt Lolly. "What's the matter?" I sat down on the floor beside her.

"I may as well tell you." She turned her face toward me and I saw that her cheeks were lined with mascara tears. Lolly only wore that stuff when she went to see Roy. "Roy's enlisted," she blurted. "The government's out to ruin my life."

"Enlisted? Like going to the army or something?"

"Yes."

"But how is the government ruining your life?" I asked. "I don't get it."

"The government's letting him enlist. Don't they know he's needed here at home to make doughnuts and run his grocery store?"

"But he doesn't make airplanes or bombs," I began. "It's not like we need doughnuts for defense." Then I decided not to say anything else. In her rickety frame of mind, she didn't need to hear me say it was okay if Roy wanted to enlist.

"He's going off to get killed before we get married and I'll wind up being an old maid forever." She choked and sputtered like the car Grandanna used to have.

"But Aunt Lolly, you're not an old maid. You're a widow for Uncle Art, remember?" I wondered if she could be a double widow or if a long engagement to Roy didn't count. But you never know with grownups, they have strange rules.

"That's just it. First a widow and then an old maid. I expected to be a bride again." Aunt Lolly sounded about as steady as a hog on ice.

Uh, oh. I shouldn't have reminded her. My mind wasn't running right with those baby boxes getting in the way of clear thinking.

"Why is she crying?" Ida Mae appeared in the attic

window, framed like a snapshot.

"Roy's going off to war," I said.

"What war?" She clambered over the sill.

"War's coming, that's what Roy says, and he's got to be there. He says he'll have to go sooner or later, so it might as well be sooner." Aunt Lolly managed all of that in one long outburst before she collapsed in a fit of sniffling.

"Ida Mae, why don't you sit down and visit with Aunt Lolly for a minute?" I felt itchy with sweat and what I might find in those boxes.

Ida Mae didn't need to be asked twice. She began to entertain Aunt Lolly with a story about her mother's latest boyfriend.

Quickly I brought one of the pink boxes into the daylight near the window and opened it. Baby clothes, just like Grandanna said. What did I expect to find, for crumb's sake? While Ida Mae rambled on, I brought the other box near the window and untied the faded ribbon around it.

Pictures! Lots and lots of pictures! Some were faded and had yellow edges, but I could still figure out the people in them. They were wearing funny clothes, so that meant the pictures must be really old. One person looked like mom, a real young mom because she said she didn't bob her hair until she was about sixteen and here, in the snapshot, her wavy, black hair was long, down to her waist. Bob, what a funny word to use for cutting your hair short.

"Maggie!"

I scrambled to my feet. Aunt Lolly wasn't crying now, she was standing right beside me and, from the way she glared, I had become her target instead of Hitler and the government.

"Aunt Lolly, I was just looking . . . "

She grabbed the box from my hands. "Leave it be. Don't be snooping in things that'll only rile everything up."

She shoved the lid down so hard I was afraid she'd break the box. Then she grabbed the box of clothes as well and put them back in the corner.

"Let's go," she said. She opened the attic door, flung the ladder into place and disappeared down it.

Ida Mae and I looked at each other.

"Now I'll never get a decent look at those pictures," I began. "She'll tell Grandanna, and I'll never be allowed up here again."

"You can look at this picture if you want to," Ida Mae said, looking like a cat in a cream house. "It just kind of flew off the floor and into my hand."

I made a grab for the yellowed snapshot, but Ida Mae's hand out-maneuvered mine.

"No, you don't." She put the picture in the pocket of her cutoffs. "You're not lookin' at this picture unless you promise to find out who the lady is in it. She's wearin' the funniest lookin' hat you ever seen."

Ida Mae disappeared down the outside ladder as her words nailed me to the spot. "Did the funny hat have a flower on it?" I called after her. Like the lady of my dreams is wearing, I added to myself.

"Ida Mae," I called, coming to life. "Wait for me."

Six

I raced to the window and watched Ida Mae disappear
around the corner of the house. She was headed for her
grandma's and knew I'd follow her because I had to see that
snapshot she grabbed from the box.

"Maggie, come down here right now."

Uh, oh. It was Grandanna calling with that funny edge
to her voice. That meant one thing. I'd better do what she
said. Probably the three of them — Aunt Bess, Aunt Lolly,
and Grandanna — were conspiring down there in the
kitchen about what they were going to do to me for getting
into the pink boxes. But I had to know what was in them.
Couldn't they understand that?

"Coming," I called, and climbed down the ladder.

Aunt Lolly wasn't around and neither was Aunt Bess. This looked bad. A one-on-one with Grandanna was worse than being called into the principal's office.

"I thought we ought to have a little chat," Grandanna began. "Just the two of us."

"Where's Aunt Lolly?"

"She's gone to a funeral. She says they always make her feel better. You know how she is."

I didn't know, but now I had to make my peace with Grandanna. "I'm really sorry I got her all upset. I didn't know she'd take Roy's enlisting so hard."

"That's not the subject of our conversation just now, although it might be next time." Grandanna sat down at the kitchen table and pointed to a chair across from her. "That's for you."

"Ida Mae's kind of expecting me," I said.

"She'll wait. This won't." Grandanna wasn't going to be detoured. "Seems like you all-of-a-sudden got a lot of questions on your mind," she began. "What brought that on?"

I began to roll up the edges of the placemat in front of me. "I . . . I'm kind of curious, you know, about things." Suddenly I got cold, shivery scared. What if I wasn't ready to hear what she had to say to me? I'd never thought of that.

"What things are you talking about? The things in those pink boxes?" Wisps of hair had escaped from her tightly-wrapped bun at the back of her head. It made her look as if she might be wired to something electrical.

I took a deep breath. "Who are all those people in those old-time snapshots?"

She sighed. "It's been ages since I had a look. Don't know if I can recollect offhand."

"I'll go get them." I bolted out of my chair and headed for the ladder to the attic.

"Hold on," she said. "I got to confer with a few people first and don't know if this is the right time for a delicate discussion about the family. You know, your mama bein' big with child and all."

The telephone rang, and Grandanna looked at me as if I had something to do with it. "Who's that?" she asked.

I shrugged, although I hoped it was Ida Mae with some plan to get me out of here.

Grandanna spoke into the telephone for a minute, then put her hand over the receiver. "Looks like I'm gonna be a while," she began. "Somebody wants me to make her a rug, and we got to talk about colors."

"I'll be in the backyard," I said.

"Don't go far. We're not done talkin' yet."

"Yes, ma'am." But I knew she'd be talking for some time. When she talks about colors and prices and sizes, she can go on for hours. The longer the talk, the longer the rug. But it's important. Outside of her widow's pension from the railroad, the rest of her bacon and eggs come from the money she gets for weaving rugs.

Ida Mae answered my knock at her grandma's back door.

"What kept you?" she asked, opening the screen door. "Thought you were so anxious to see this here picture."

I explained about Grandanna as I looked around the dark, messy kitchen that smelled of grease. I hoped I was never invited to supper.

"Who's there, Ida Mae?" a voice called from another part of the house.

"Maggie Calhoun," Ida Mae shouted. "It's Grandma," she whispered to me.

"I'll be there in a minute," Mrs. Dean said.

"Ida Mae, let me have the snapshot. I have to get right back because Grandanna's waiting to talk to me. I'll tell you what she says about the picture, honest I will."

"But you got to say hi to my grandma first." Ida Mae was sure enjoying the power she held over me right now. "You're not scared of her, are you?"

"No, I have to go right back, that's all."

Mrs. Dean swept into the room like some old time movie star. She headed straight for me, her scarves and long gray hair fluttering all around as if she'd been caught in a high wind.

"Maggie Calhoun, let me look at you." She grabbed my face and stared hard. "I sense your longing to know more about the past," she began.

"Huh?"

"Your aura seeks answers," she continued.

"Scuse me?" I looked into her dark eyes ringed by lines of black makeup. She reminded me of the wicked witch of the west in *The Wizard of Oz*. After I saw that show last winter, Judy Garland became my all time favorite movie star.

"Grandma, me and Maggie have to go," Ida Mae said.

"In a minute." Mrs. Dean grabbed my hand. "Let me see your wart, darling."

"Ida Mae's already told me what to do," I said. "Rub a chicken gizzard on it."

"But did she tell you when?" She leaned down close to me and the smell of spicy incense surrounded my nose. Mom always burns that stuff when the sewer backs up.

"By the light of a full moon preferably," she said, without waiting for an answer. "Rub the gizzard on your wart by the light of a full moon. If the moon isn't full, it may take longer for the wart to fall off. Then bury the gizzard, but don't tell where or the spell will be broken."

"Yes, ma'am, right, okay." I slowly pulled my hand from hers. "Thanks a lot, Mrs. Dean. I really have to go now. Bye. Bye, Ida Mae."

I ran towards Grandanna's hedge, remembering now why I never wanted to go to Mrs. Dean's except at Halloween. The rest of the year I didn't like to be that spooked by anybody.

"Maggie, wait." Ida Mae was coming.

"Give me that picture, then leave me alone," I shouted, turning on her.

"Grandma don't mean nothing by her act," Ida Mae said. "She says the ladies at church stopped invited her to circle meetings when she started wearing funny makeup, and that's the best thing that's ever happened to her."

"Just give me what's mine."

"I'm not sure where I put it," she said, but her cocky grin told me otherwise.

"Ida Mae, I just got tired of you and your shenanigans. From now on, leave me alone. There's bound to be another picture of that lady somewheres, and when I find out who she is, you'll be the last person in the world to know." I turned and ran for Grandanna's, then slammed the back door in Ida Mae's face. Boy, did that feel good.

A strange man stood in Grandanna's parlor talking to her.

They both turned to look at me now as I walked slowly towards them.

"Is this the little lady we been talking about, Anna?" The man asked Grandanna. He was big and hefty, and when he held out his hand to shake mine I noticed his pinky finger had a ring on it set with a shiny stone that was big enough to choke a horse.

"Yes, this is my granddaughter, Maggie," Grandanna said in a kind of company best voice. "Honey, this here's Punch Hardaway, my insurance man."

"No one has endurance like the man who sells insurance," he laughed, still shaking my hand.

"Yes sir," I answered, mystified about what he'd said. In fact, today was turning out to be a day when people were saying things that just didn't make sense.

"Grandanna, I think I better go home to Uncle Dick's. Seems like we had something planned for tonight."

"We'll finish our talk tomorrow," she said, giving me a knowing look.

I said my goodbyes and headed down the sidewalk, past Mrs. Dean's, then Frank Cunningham's, and the vacant lot on the corner. I saw Uncle Dick walking towards me, crossing the street at the intersection ahead.

"Uncle Dick," I shouted, hurrying up to him. "You're

home early."

He gave me a hug as we met each other in the middle of the block.

"I got done early so thought I'd come home and spend a little time with you," he said. We walked in silence for a minute or two, but I felt that Uncle Dick had something he wanted to say. I'm sure that Aunt Bess had already gotten in her two cents' worth about me and the boxes.

"Grandanna wanted to talk to me about something special," I began. Then I told him everything that happened, finishing up with Punch Hardaway. "He called me a little lady, Uncle Dick, and I got out of there because I hate it when somebody says that."

"Maggie, sometimes we have to hear things that we don't always understand at first and we need to have a little conversation about that." He paused. "Punch was at Grandanna's, you say? I wonder what that was all about."

"And he said this funny thing about insurance," I said. "I don't get it."

"Neither do I," said Uncle Dick. "Neither do I."

I knew though, that he was thinking about something else entirely.

Seven

A couple of mornings later I woke up to hear Aunt Bess and Uncle Dick talking. Aunt Bess could be heard on Main Street if Oquawka had a Main Street, but Uncle Dick was just answering in grunts and growls.

"You're eavesdripping," Cooper said, his voice muffled by bed covers.

"Eavesdropping, but I'm not. I'm just . . . just stretching." Then I stretched, but I didn't convince him, or me for that matter. But I'd heard my name and Punch Hardaway's and Mom and Dad's all rolled up into one sentence. None of it made sense, but when Aunt Bess was talking her brain moved faster than her tongue.

"I'm hungry," Cooper announced and threw back his

covers. The voices in the dining room stopped as if a radio had been turned off.

"Now see what you did," I whispered.

Cooper only grinned and hurried down the hall to the bathroom.

By the time I was dressed and ready for breakfast, Cooper was already eating bacon and eggs. Aunt Bess was ironing Uncle Dick's socks. "Good morning, Maggie," she said. "Want the same as Cooper?"

"Think I'll just have cereal," I said. "I'll get it."

"Got plans to be with Ida Mae today?" Aunt Bess held up a sock with a big hole in it and threw it back in the clothes basket.

"No." I stuffed my mouth with Rice Krispies so I wouldn't have to say any more.

"Betcha you and Ida Mae had another fight," Cooper said. "About that picture she stole." His big, messy grin made me mad enough to spit nails.

"How do you know?" I began, then stopped quickly. Aunt Bess was staring at us, and I figured this could be trouble.

"Thought you and Grandanna had a little conversation about that business," she said. She was ironing the same sock over and over.

"Didn't quite get to it, Aunt Bess. She got a phone call and then . . . "

"Oh, yes, I remember." She ironed some more before she went on. "But you need to talk to her, Maggie, you really do. Or maybe . . . " She stopped and sudden tears made pools in her eyes.

"Where's Uncle Dick?" Cooper asked, standing up.

"He's upstairs in the attic doing bills, but I expect you could interrupt him if it's really important." Aunt Bess went back to ironing after wiping her nose on an embroidered handkerchief. "Doing bills isn't his favorite sport."

"Excuse me." Cooper left his eggy dishes on the table and ran from the room. He hated to see grownups use emotions that were supposed to be reserved for kids. Like crying.

I stared out of the window at the beautiful sunny morning, thoughts flying through my head. Now, in the sudden quiet after Cooper left, I had a chance to sort through my thoughts, wondering. Why was Aunt Bess getting all weepy again? And why did I have to have a heart-to-heart with Grandanna? We talked all the time anyways, so what was so important about getting all formal about it? And Mom? How much longer would it be until the new baby came and we moved to California? Suddenly my life had become so worrisome.

"Maggie."

"What is it, Aunt Bess?"

"You seem kind of worried, moody even."

"It's just . . . just . . . I don't know. Sometimes I wish I could be a little kid again, Cooper's age maybe, so I wouldn't have to do anything but play. And then I feel old, worrying about stuff I can't even put a name to. All I want to know . . . "

I stopped, puzzled. What did I want to know? Why couldn't I be satisfied with what I knew now? Wasn't that enough? Maybe that's all there was.

"Maggie." Aunt Bess came over and put an arm around my shoulders. "You're at an age when things are changing inside as well as out. Before long, you're going to be a young lady." She sounded as if she wanted to be somewhere else so she didn't have to deliver this message.

"Are you talking about me getting the curse?" I asked, smiling inside as I saw the shocked look on her face. "It's all right, Aunt Bess. The girls in my class talked about it at school. Then I went home and asked Mom if it was true, and she told me everything."

"I declare," she said, wiping her face again. "You children shouldn't be talking about things like that among yourselves. Next thing you know you'll be talking about . . .

well, something else you shouldn't be talking about."

I stood up and carried the breakfast dishes to the sink. "Aunt Bess, I think you've burned Uncle Dick's sock." Smoke curled up from the ironing board.

"Oh, no," she cried, lifting the iron from the cremated sock. "I never was very good at this homemaking business. I should have stuck to being a secretary to the judge. That was something I could do." She looked about ready to cry again.

"It's okay, Aunt Bess. Honest." I took the iron from her and she sat down. "Can I do anything else?" I tried to iron but made wrinkles instead.

"Well, let's see. You can go to the store if you want. Thought I'd ask Grandanna and Lolly over for supper tonight. Fried chicken is Lolly's favorite, and she needs cheering up."

Chicken. Chicken gizzards. I could tell Ida Mae I'd rubbed one on my wart if I decided to go through with that stupid idea. Then I remembered I wasn't speaking to her.

"I'll go. Make out a list."

Cooper was playing Monopoly with Uncle Dick when I left, so I went by myself. I wasn't alone very long. Ida Mae appeared out of nowhere. She must have learned how to do that from her Grandma Dean.

"Where you headed?" she asked, keeping pace beside me.

"The grocery store. Not that it's any of your beeswax."

"You're still mad?"

"Give me one good reason why I shouldn't be."

"Here's the picture you're so all fired up to see." She handed me the snapshot she'd grabbed in Grandma's attic a few days ago. "Now you got no reason to be mad. None at all."

I stopped to look at the picture. Those faces leaped out at me. My very young mom, I was sure of it. And maybe Aunt Bess, except her hair was dark and long, not like now, short and almost gray. There was a young man standing next to Aunt Bess. Could that be Uncle Dick? It was hard to tell because the picture was so blurry. But I'd know the hat on the lady next to him, the hat of my dreams. Big, black, and shading the face of the person wearing it.

"Want to come over for fried chicken tonight?" I asked Ida Mae, feeling friendly towards her again.

"Sure." She gave a little skip. "At least I'll recognize what I'm eating. Never know what Grandma feeds me, it don't look like nothing I ever saw before."

"Maybe it's chicken gizzards."

"Ick," she said, pretending to gag.

"Maybe she thinks your stomach is full of warts."

"Oh, double ick." Now she hit my arm and I hit her

back. Being with Ida Mae could sure take your mind off your troubles — if she wasn't the one causing them.

Just before we went into the store, I said, "Thanks, Ida Mae, for giving me the picture."

"It's okay," she shrugged. "I was afraid you were going to be mad forever. You're my only friend, and without you I wouldn't have nobody."

Later, as we walked home with the grocery sacks, Ida Mae asked, "Are you gonna do it tonight?"

"Do what?"

"You know." She sounded exasperated. "Rub the gizzard on your wart by the light of the moon. I heard you ask Roy to wrap it up special, separate from the rest of the chicken."

I shifted the grocery sack I carried from one arm to the other. "I haven't decided yet. It probably won't work anyways."

"Every goofy thing my grandma believes in works. I told you, she's got the gift." Ida Mae sounded a little goofy herself right now. "But you got to believe."

At home I hid the chicken gizzard in the freezer behind the corn and the peas. Then we helped Aunt Bess make two more cherry pies and picked weeds for salad. She showed us how to make yeast biscuits too, and even let us punch the dough down twice.

At five o'clock Grandanna called and asked Uncle Dick to pick her up because her bunions were killing her. Fifteen minutes later we all sat at the kitchen table. Lolly seemed cheered up today and told us about a funeral she'd attended.

We washed and dried the dishes, then all sat on the front porch and watched the sky burn itself up in a dark, red sunset. Uncle Dick brought his guitar, tuned it up, and we all joined in singing the songs we loved best — "Blue Tail Fly," "On Top of Old Smoky," and "Red River Valley." He always saved "Amazing Grace" for last, so when he strummed the opening chords, I knew the concert was nearly over. Grandanna sighed, and when she stood up she swayed like a bush reed in backwater. She got skinnier by the day.

"Dick, do you mind taking Grandanna home?" Lolly asked. "Thought I'd just drop by the store and see if Roy needs any help making doughnuts tonight."

"I'll take you," he said. "Come on, Ida Mae. I can drop you off with Grandanna. Bess, I'm gonna stop by the Odd Fellows and play a few hands of cards. Be home by 9:30 at the latest."

While the grownups were saying goodbye, Ida Mae winked and blinked at me as if she was one of those signal things on a ship. Guess she was trying to say something about later tonight.

She wasn't going with me though. I was going alone. But what was I trying to prove? That I was a big girl and could go outside in the dark all by myself? No, something else was at work here, something I couldn't figure. It must be the changing going on inside me. Maybe it was all a part of growing up, suddenly noticing the world is bigger, lots bigger than the one I was used to.

But first, I had to get rid of my wart.

Eight

By ten o'clock, everyone was asleep. Except me, of course. I could hear Uncle Dick's steady snores from upstairs and Cooper's puffy little snorts in the bed across from mine. It sounded as if a family of piglets had decided to spend the night. Slipping out of bed, I grabbed my shoes and tiptoed into the kitchen. Underneath my pajamas I still wore my shorts and blouse. I took off my jams, took the gizzard bag from the freezer, and quietly closed the back door behind me as I left.

It was darker than I thought it would be. If there was a moon, it sure was being shy. Maybe it would come up later and maybe it wouldn't come up at all. That says a lot about my belief in Mrs. Dean's so-called gift. The moon was supposed to be so important to this craziness of Mrs. Dean's, yet I didn't even know what size the moon would be tonight. I didn't know if it would even be big enough to make a glow so I could bury the gizzard by its light and have my wart drop off in a few days.

I stood on the back porch for a while, waiting to see if anyone had heard me. If Uncle Dick or Aunt Bess found me out of bed, I could say that I had a stomachache. But Uncle Dick would see right through that. I had my street clothes on, so he'd figure I was going somewhere. And going somewhere by myself at ten o'clock at night would not be on his list of things for me to do even though he understands kids better than any grownup I know.

So why was I doing this? I hated my wart. Anything was worth a try to get rid of it, even trying something I wasn't sure would work. But Ida Mae believed in her grandma's power, and that's all I needed. "Okay, wart, you've got to go," I whispered.

Now where, that was the next question. In our backyard would be the first place anyone would guess, especially Ida Mae. But where wouldn't she guess in a million years? That didn't take long. I headed for her backyard.

A few houses still had lights shining from their bedroom windows to keep me company as I walked along the dark streets. Oquawka wasn't big enough to have more than about ten streets that were important enough for streetlights, and this wasn't one of them. So I walked along in the dark.

"We're getting closer, wart," I whispered. My voice gave me a little comfort and lots of company.

I told myself that I wasn't scared. After all, I walked these two blocks every day when I came to visit. I knew every tree, every bush, every brick in the sidewalk, especially those that had cracks in them. Shade trees, elms, maples, and a pine or two thrown in were as protective as Grandanna's big, black umbrella. Their shadows were mostly friendly, except when they looked like the shadows in my nightmares.

Funny, I hadn't thought about those nightmares in a long time. I used to have them, sometimes a couple of times a week when I was little. Then they sort of disappeared. It was always the same dream. Someone would come in the night, usually when rain and leaves scratched my window. I used to think there were special nightmare trees that grew leaves with fingernails on them. Then that someone would take me out of my bed, down the steps to the front door, and . . . and then I woke up. The nightmare ended there as I woke up screaming the house awake.

Suddenly I shuddered on that quiet, dark street in Oquawka. Why did I have to think of that stupid dream now? There was nothing to be scared of.

"Think of something else," I told myself.

A car veered around the corner, its headlights nearly catching me in their bright cones. I ducked behind a tree and waited for it to pass. Was it Uncle Dick looking for me? No, he would have used his truck.

"Relax," I said aloud. "He doesn't know you've gone."

I continued walking, first to the intersection, then turning on the street where Grandanna and Mrs. Dean and Frank Cunningham lived. Frank's house was dark, but hardly quiet. As I came closer, I heard him playing "Oh, Johnny, How You Can Love." Practicing, I thought, practicing in the dark. For a couple of minutes I stopped to listen. I could listen in the dark, too.

The next house was Mrs. Dean's, looming suddenly like a dark rock on a distant plain. Someone had built so many nooks and crannies and additions to the house that it looked as if it had once been hot lava cooled to this gigantic blob.

I tiptoed towards the backyard, praying I wouldn't step on something that would make a noise. Maybe Mrs. Dean had traps set for animals or other live things, or considering her frame of mind, for dead things as well. Could you catch a ghost with a bear trap? It was such a crazy idea that she might believe it.

I was halfway around the house before I noticed the car parked in front of Grandanna's two doors down. A small light shone in her living room and bedroom. Why would she be having company at this hour? Maybe it was Aunt Lolly's company instead. Maybe Roy had taken her home and they were carrying on in the living room. But I thought you turned the lights out to kiss and hug, at least that's how they show it in the movies.

I crept from tree to hedge and tree again, until I reached the walk to Grandanna's front porch. There was nothing else to do but walk straight ahead and hope that no one came out while I was there. I made it to the lilac bush before I heard voices and the screen door squeaked open.

"Don't wait so long to call next time, Anna," a man's voice said as he stepped out on the porch. "You can't let yourself run out of those pills."

"Grandanna," I wanted to call out. "What's wrong? Are you sick?" But I couldn't. If she knew I was out alone after dark, she'd be so upset that I'd only make her feel worse.

"Didn't seem like it was gonna be my ruination this time." Grandanna's voice was barely audible. "But I hear you, Bathless. I'll fill the prescription you gave me cuz I got unfinished business to attend to before I go."

Bathless. That was old Doc Grogan she was talking to! He got his nickname when he was a kid and never washed up much. Old timers, like Grandanna, had never called him by his rightful name. What was he doing here at this time of night? She must have had a bad spell when she got home after supper at our house. Come to think of it, she ate a fair amount of watermelon pickles.

Doc Grogan climbed in his car and drove down the street. I stayed and watched as Grandanna turned out the lights in the living room, then soon after, the light in her bedroom. Aunt Lolly didn't appear so she must still be out with Roy, hugging and kissing somewhere else.

I walked around to the backyard and crawled through the hedge to the neighbor's, then through the next hedge into Mrs. Dean's. A dog barked down the street, and I waited. He couldn't know I was here, but he might wake up somebody who'd get curious. No one showed up though, no lights clicked on inside or out.

Now where should I bury this gizzard anyway? It was beginning to thaw in the package, getting all squishy inside and I couldn't wait to get rid of it.

I peered into the darkness. There was a path toward the tool shed and a rhubarb patch just beyond.

The dirt was still soft from the rain as I dug. Suddenly, I heard a sound, a scrape or scratch of wood on brick. It happened so fast, I didn't have time to react.

"Who is it?" a raspy voice demanded. "Who's on my property?" A hand grabbed my shoulder and pulled me erect.

"What have we here?" I could smell that spicy incense perfume she wore, even before I saw her faint outline against the shed.

"It's me, Mrs. Dean," I whispered. "It's Maggie Calhoun."

"That isn't your name," she whispered back fiercely. "I know your real name."

"It is too my real name." My voice grew louder now, more insistent. What was the matter with her? She knew who I was.

"No, no, it isn't, child. Why doesn't someone tell you everything? It's time for the truth to come out."

I pulled away from her. If there was truth to be found out, I didn't want to hear it from her.

Then I was running through her yard, down the front sidewalk and then the block, past Frank Cunningham's house towards the corner. As I ran, the sound of a dog's bark followed my steps, and a light clicked on in the house on the corner. I crossed the street to hide in the shadow of an elm to catch my breath.

Then I felt that awful squishy gizzard again. I'd taken it out of the package to bury it, and now I still held its soft, sliminess in my hand. I threw it as far as I could, hearing it land in a bush nearby. I couldn't wait to wipe my hand on my blouse, feeling the wart catch on a bit of trim on the pocket.

"Get used to it, wart," I whispered. "You're gonna be there for a long time."

Slowly I walked home, feeling trembly inside and out, hoping that Uncle Dick would be waiting for me with big hugs and an explanation for all this. There was no question now. I hadn't made up my funny feelings that made me wonder who I was. But if I wasn't Maggie Calhoun, like Mrs. Dean said, then who was I?

Nine

I ran the rest of the way home. Just before I went inside, I stopped to catch my breath. My heart was pounding faster than a horse can trot, and it sounded loud enough to wake up all those folks laid out in Restful Sleep Cemetery north of town.

For a second I'd almost wanted Uncle Dick to be standing on the front porch, rocking back and forth on his heels, waiting for me to explain what I was doing out alone after dark. It would be easier if he were waiting to talk. Then maybe I could get the words out and ask what Mrs. Dean meant. He always seemed to know about everything.

I eased in the back door and tiptoed into the sunroom. Cooper wasn't snoring any more and hardly moved as I settled in my own bed without bothering to change back into my pajamas. The moon had finally made a slivery appearance and I could see Cooper's profile. His goofy turned-up nose looked as if it had been carved from Ivory soap.

Just before I fell asleep, I thought I heard a little clicking noise coming from somewhere in the house. Just a click, then I dropped into sleep with no time to think about what had happened tonight. Maybe I had already started to dream on my way to sleep. Maybe all of tonight would become part of a dream that I'd remember only briefly before it disappeared in the morning.

But it didn't disappear. Even before I opened my eyes, I remembered in a flash seeing Grandanna talking with old Doc Grogan, and then hearing those awful words of Mrs. Dean's over and over. "Your name isn't Maggie Calhoun," she'd said. "Your name isn't Maggie Calhoun."

I heard a little snuffle, a slight cough, and then felt a spidery breath on my cheeks.

"Morning, Cooper."

"How did you know I was standing here?" he whispered. "Your eyes are still closed."   ”

"I had a hunch."

"Did you have a bedtime snack after I went to bed?" I

could feel Cooper examining my face closely.

"No."

"How come your face is dirty then? Bet you're telling me a fib."

"Cross my heart, I didn't."

"Liar, liar, pants on fire," he whispered.

"Cooper . . . " I sounded a warning note.

"Well, okay then. Uncle Dick said to tell him when you woke up."

"You can go tell him now."

"Okay."

I listened as his feet padded across the bare floor to the living room carpet. When I couldn't hear him any more, I opened my eyes. The sunshine flooding the room surprised me. I'd halfway expected the day to look like my insides felt. Gray, cloudy, chance of rain. Any second I felt I would burst out crying. Suddenly I felt so much older, so full of feelings that didn't make sense. I thought it got easier as you grew up, that you were smarter and always knew the answers to everything. It isn't fair, I wanted to yell out to somebody. Nobody has a choice about growing up. You have to do it, so why does it have to be so hard?

I felt last night's clothes twisted around on me and jumped up, grabbed clean shorts and a knit top, and ran to the bathroom. I passed Cooper who had stopped to examine a bug he'd found on the living room carpet.

"You must have to go bad," he called after me.

Quickly, I changed and washed my face. Good thing, too. Dirt stained both my clothes and skin, and there was a big spot on my blouse where I'd held the chicken gizzard too close before I threw it away. I swallowed hard and for a second thought I'd have the dry heaves. Finally, everything settled down and I could face the morning.

Aunt Bess and Uncle Dick were sitting at the breakfast table when I walked into the kitchen. Just sitting, not drinking coffee, not eating their pancakes, not even listening to the morning Hog and Steer Report on the radio that just sat up there on the shelf above the stove talking to itself.

"Guess I slept a little late." I tried to make my voice sound light but it came out squeaky, like a toy.

"Good morning." Uncle Dick tried to sound cheery as well, but his eyes sent a different message. Uh, oh. He probably heard me come in last night. Uncle Dick didn't miss much.

"We need to start thinking about the fish fry." The words flew out of Aunt Bess like a horse out of a starting gate. "Got to get Grandanna to do some serious fishing for us."

"Oh, no," I cried out. "She can't do that, it's too . . . "

Then I stopped. Did they know she was taking real pills that the doctor gave her, not just store-bought stuff? And how would I explain that I knew this?

"Why can't she?" Aunt Bess stared at me, her dark eyes as bright as a sparrow's.

"Well, I figured maybe she needed help or something," I mumbled. Cooper ambled into the room before they had a chance to ask another question.

"You look better now that your face is clean," he said to me. Then he turned to Aunt Bess and Uncle Dick. "You should have seen her," he began.

"Cooper, I've got an idea," I interrupted. "Wouldn't you like to go fishing with me? I'll carry the poles and the bait cans, and even pull you in the wagon."

"I'd rather go with Uncle Dick," he said. "You make me put the worms on the hook by myself, Maggie. And I hate it because they go all squishy."

"That settles it." Uncle Dick stood up and carried his still full plate to the sink.

"Cooper, you and I will go. We didn't catch a thing the other day. We got to show those fish who's the boss."

"Boys only, right, Uncle Dick?" Cooper asked.

"Boys only," Uncle Dick answered, winking at me.

Cooper started undressing before he left the room, a big

smile spreading like melted butter across his face. "Be right back," he said.

After he left Aunt Bess and Uncle Dick and I looked at each other as if we'd just met. Suddenly I blurted out, "I'm sorry," and burst into tears.

Uncle Dick put his arms around me and hugged hard. "It's okay, sweetheart, it's okay. Cry till you get it all out."

"Is there something you want to tell us?" Aunt Bess asked.

"No." I rubbed my face against Uncle Dick's shirt. "I mean yes. Last night I went out to bury a chicken gizzard, and Mrs. Dean found me and then she said . . . "

"Don't say another word," Aunt Bess answered. "That woman is crazier than a coot. You can't pay any attention to what she says. But what about that chicken gizzard thing? Land sakes, did she tell you to do that?"

"No, Ida Mae did."

"I declare," Aunt Bess shook her head. "It runs in the family."

"No, it's not Ida Mae's fault. She's not to blame," I burst out. "But somebody is."

Aunt Bess glanced up at Uncle Dick with a face I'd never seen before. Someone else was looking out of her eyes.

"Maggie, let's you and me go upstairs and have a little

talk," Uncle Dick said. "Tell Cooper I'll be right down, Bess."

I followed him upstairs to his office. He sat down at his desk which was really an old pine door sitting on a couple of sawhorses. Stacks of papers, three boxes of nails, and his black telephone covered most of the space on it. He was so happy when he got his dial phone a few years back. He said then that he didn't have to talk to that nosy Mrs. Granger down at the telephone exchange any more. He said she ought to be called the gossip exchange instead.

I stared at the calendar from Hillard Lochinvar's Feed and Seed store nailed to the wall behind him. "Uncle Dick, your calendar says January 1941."

He turned around and looked at it. "Guess I'm about six months late," he said. He yanked off five pages and threw them in a box he used for a wastebasket.

Six months ago I was still a kid. I didn't know Mom was going to have a baby. I didn't know we were going to move to California. And I didn't know there was something else to know about me.

"Uncle Dick," I began. "Is there something wrong with me? Is that why people are saying things, or not saying things?"

"Honey, there's nothing wrong with you." Uncle Dick's

voice sounded soothing and warm. "But I know something's been bothering you, so that's why I wanted to talk. I think it's high time to say that you are a wonderful little girl, and you ought not to worry about yourself so much. Just remember that we all love you." He picked up a pencil stub as if he planned to write the rest of his talk to me. "Does that help?"

I nodded, but it didn't, not really. Uncle Dick was being nice having this talk with me, but he wasn't saying anything. There's such a big difference. I tried not to be too disappointed before it dawned on me that, maybe, Uncle Dick didn't know what was going on either.

The telephone on his desk began to ring, its tone shrill and demanding as if Mrs. Granger was still in charge of it.

"Yes?" Uncle Dick said into the receiver. He listened, then put a hand over the mouthpiece and looked at me. "This will take a couple of minutes, Maggie."

"Okay." I left the room, walked out to the main part of the attic and sat down on an old trunk. I sighed and felt my tight, wound up feeling kind of melt. Grandanna wanted to talk to me too. Maybe she would have more to say than Uncle Dick.

Things were a lot neater up here in Aunt Bess's attic than they were in Grandanna's. Aunt Bess had lined up some cardboard boxes, each one neatly marked with what was inside them. "Dress Patterns and Old Fabric" was one. That didn't sound too interesting. "Sheet Music 1930-1935" read another. Mom used to play the piano, so maybe that was her box. Another small box in a corner read "Legal Papers." Ida Mae would really wonder about that.

Away off in another corner a large box sat alone. I walked over to it and read its label — "Costumes." Costumes for what?

"Maggie." Uncle Dick called to me. "Oh, there you are," he said, walking over to where I stood. "Honey, I can't stay and talk any more just now. Something's come up and I have to go to town right away. That phone call was from the bank, and there's a chance I may not get a loan I was counting on."

"A loan? Like in money?"

"Yes." Uncle Dick cleared his throat a couple of times. "You see, things are a little tight right now. I have to borrow some cash to pay for the cost of moving that house. You know, pay for permits to the county, and to the man who's going to help me. In the meantime, I have to wait thirty days to get paid for my work, so I have a little problem just now with having enough . . . enough cash. Nothing for you to worry about though."

"Oh, I see." But I really didn't. I'd never thought of

Uncle Dick needing money because he always seemed to have enough for him and Aunt Bess and anyone else who needed help. Maybe the hard times Dad talked about had finally arrived on Uncle Dick's doorstep too.

"First, though, I have to tell Cooper I can't take him fishing like I promised. I know he'll be disappointed, so maybe you'd help by taking him to Highlander's for some ice cream. I've got two nickels here that will buy two double-decker cones for my two favorite kids."

"Okay, and thanks, Uncle Dick. And thanks for talking to me too."

Uncle Dick hurried downstairs while I stayed in the shadowed corner of the attic. I tried to be satisfied that he had told me everything I needed to know. Oh, why couldn't I rip off some pages of a calendar just like he did and be the same person that I used to be — Maggie Calhoun, Ordinary Girl?

Ten

I tried to stay out of everyone's way for a couple of days, and the grownups almost acted relieved. They behaved as if they'd forgotten the questions that needed answering, and I didn't know how to get them to remembering. It was all an act though. I knew that. Nobody wanted to say anything because it would make everyone uncomfortable. Even Ida Mae hadn't come over, and she usually thrived on uncomfortable. If she'd had any other grandma, I would have gone to her house or called her. But no way did I want to come face to face with Mrs. Dean, in person or on the telephone. She gave me the willies even when I just thought about her.

And then a shiver ran through my brain. She was the one

who said I wasn't Maggie Calhoun. Was it worth the risk to ask her questions that my relatives wouldn't or couldn't answer and find out why she spoke those awful words? Was she talking because she knew things or just because she was crazy, like Aunt Bess said?

Aunt Bess was in the kitchen shelling peas and listening to "Our Gal Sunday" on the radio when I headed for the back door.

"I'm going for a walk," I told her. "If I see Ida Mae, I might bring her back. Is that okay?"

"That's a good idea," she said. "Just don't bother Grandanna right now. She told me she was going to take a nap this afternoon. Been working too hard on a rug she's making for Mrs. Phipps."

I closed the screen door without banging it and headed toward Second Street. Cooper had gone out to play with a boy in the neighborhood, and I hoped he was leaving Grandanna alone as well. Soon I was walking past Frank Cunningham's house and then the overgrown strawberry patch in the vacant lot. A minute later I was standing in front of Mrs. Dean's.

I drew in a huge bite of air and knocked on the front door. Ida Mae jerked it open before I had time to change my mind.

"Hey," she said, opening the screen door. "Come on in."

Her hair looked like a gritty tumbleweed, and her clothes were dirty enough to stand alone.

"Why don't you come outside instead?" I backed down a couple of steps off the porch.

"Grandma's not home," she said. "So you don't need to worry about running into her." But she came out to stand on the porch anyway.

"Have you been sick?" I asked. "I haven't seen you for a couple of days."

"Been helping Grandma clean closets. She said it was about time I earned my keep." Ida Mae looked at her hands and so did I. Each fingernail was outlined in dirt.

"Closets must be pretty dirty."

"Don't have to get snotty about it." She put her hands behind her back. "But you're right, those closets hadn't been cleaned since Hector was a pup. No wonder my mom ran away from home. I would too, if I lived here." Ida Mae stared off down the street, her face crumpled like tissue paper on Christmas morning.

"But you do live here, Ida Mae," I reminded her. "At least for the summer."

Ida Mae turned her fierce gaze on me, then wiped her face causing a faint line of dirt to travel from her nose to one eye. "I don't live anywhere," she said. "Mom wants me to stay here, and Grandma says I have to go back to Peoria 'cause I interfere with her spirits. She says they won't communicate with her as long as I stay. As soon as I get the closets done, I have to go."

Maybe I'm not so bad off, I thought, before the shivers started in on me again and I backed down another step. That decided it. No way did I want to talk to Mrs. Dean about anything. "I'm going home," I began. "I think Aunt Bess wants me to help fix supper."

"But it isn't lunchtime yet." Ida Mae said.

"We start supper early."

"I could go with you," Ida Mae said in a kind of little girl voice. "I'm a good helper."

I stared at her. Ida Mae's main talent was getting in the way, but right now she wanted to abandon this house as much as I did. "Okay, come on. Let's go. Maybe Aunt Bess will let us look at some of the stuff in the attic before we start supper."

Ida Mae slammed the door behind her. "What stuff?" she asked as we started down the street.

I told her about the labeled boxes, and she began to smile. "Wonder what's in the box of papers?"

I smiled. "I knew you were going to say that. I'd rather

try on the costumes."

Ida Mae smiled back. "I knew you were going to say that too."

I wondered if we were going to be best friends since we could practically read each other's minds. I wouldn't have picked her out for mine in a million years, but you just never know how the best friend thing works.

Aunt Bess was still in the kitchen listening to "The Romance of Helen Trent" and ironing when we walked in. "Hello, Ida Mae," she said. "You girls are just in time to stir up a batch of brownies. Maybe you ought to wash your hands first," she said, looking at Ida Mae's.

"Are we having company?" I asked, going to the sink.

"Ida Mae, if she wants," Aunt Bess said. "And probably Grandanna, too. She's too tired to cook these days."

"Where's Aunt Lolly?" I asked. "Why can't she ever do anything?"

"She took the bus to Galesburg to look for a job." Aunt Bess carefully ironed the dishtowels as she answered. "With Roy going to the draft, I think she's about decided to move away and get on with her life."

"What are we having for supper tonight?" Ida Mae asked, looking around for clues.

"I thought I'd fry some cats," Aunt Bess said.

"What? " Ida Mae nearly choked on the word. "Fry some cats?"

"Yes." Aunt Bess started to iron Uncle Dick's underwear. "Haven't you ever eaten catfish before?"

"No." Ida Mae shook her tumbleweed hair. "I've heard about them though."

I pulled a mixing bowl and brownie ingredients out of the cupboard, and while we mixed and measured Aunt Bess kept up a running gab on how to fry catfish. She told us about nine times to make sure, I guess, that we could do it in case a natural disaster happened and she'd be struck down before suppertime.

After we put the brownies in the oven, Aunt Bess said it was okay if we went upstairs to the attic and looked around.

"Don't make a mess," she called after us. "And don't get in the box with the legal stuff in it. That's none of your beeswax."

Thunder rumbled not far off as we climbed the steps. "Shoot," Ida Mae said. "Maybe we could just take a peek in that box anyways."

"No, we have to do like Aunt Bess said."

The attic felt stuffy and close, the air heavy with heat and humidity. Rain soon, I thought as we surveyed the scene.

"Let's look at the costumes," I said, heading for the far corner.

"Wait." Ida Mae sat down on the top step. "I want to tell you something."

"What?" I sat down beside her. Ida Mae seemed so different today, more serious or grown up, or something.

"Promise you won't tell," she began.

"Promise."

"I'm going to run away, just like my mom did."

"You can't do that."

"Yes, I can. Who's to stop me? Who cares anyways?" She stared at me with those faded blue eyes until I had to look away.

Finally, I said, "I care, Ida Mae."

That stopped her for a second, but only a second. "You're the only one."

"Aunt Bess and Uncle Dick would care too, if they knew."

"But you said you wouldn't tell."

"And I won't." But I wasn't sure if I could keep my promise. "Where would you go if you leave?"

She shrugged. "Not to Mom, that's for sure. Say, are you asking just so you can tell Grandma where to find me?"

"No, I wouldn't tell your grandma anything."

She grinned. "Good idea. She probably wouldn't believe

you anyways."

A spear of lightning suddenly threatened to cut the house in half, then a roar of thunder quickly followed. We jumped up and ran to a corner of the attic and crouched by the box labeled "Costumes."

"I'm scared," Ida Mae said after another crash of thunder boomed nearby.

"Let's do something," I said. "Let's take our minds off things." I didn't want to think about Ida Mae running away or her grandma's bad words. "Let's look in the costume box. Come on, it'll be fun."

Ida Mae watched while I opened the box and looked inside. Odors drifted out — powder smells, sweaty body smells, and cigarette smells, too.

"P. U.," Ida Mae said, holding her nose. "Those clothes stink."

Aunt Bess had never smoked as far as I knew, and judging by the unopened cigars in Uncle Dick's truck, he hadn't either. But someone had, someone had been around these costumes and smoked like a chimney.

I pulled out a short skirt, blouse, and sash in bright red, green, and blue. Aunt Bess must have worn them because they were so small. Next I pulled out a man's knee-length pants, shirt, and sash in matching colors.

"What are they for?" Ida Mae asked.

I pulled out more stuff; earrings, headscarves, black eye patches, wooden swords and black boots made out of oilcloth, like Grandanna's kitchen table cover.

"Pirates!" we both yelled at the same time. "Pirate costumes!"

"Let's try them on." Ida Mae grabbed up parts of the smaller costume and shook them out. "Hey, I think I can wear this little one. I'll be the girl pirate."

I took the rest, turned my back, and stripped down to my underwear. The shirt and pants parts were way too big for me, but I folded them over and used the big wide sash to hold them together. Then I noticed a big rip on one side of the shirt and a stain down the side of the pants. Funny that Aunt Bess kept this costume without fixing it.

Ida Mae dressed in the girl's costume and, when we both turned and looked at each other, we started to laugh. We put on our fake boots and the head wraps, then began to fence with the wooden swords that someone had painted in gold. The harder we fenced, the more we laughed, crashing into boxes and trunks all over the attic. Maybe it wasn't that funny, but we both needed to laugh and we did, as if we were driving away demons by our noise.

"Hey, can I play too?" Cooper appeared on the stairs and

watched us for a moment before he came all the way into the attic. "Where'd you get those costumes?" he asked. "I want one."

He saw our piles of clothes by the open costume box. Without waiting, he ran over and began to pull out other bright materials. Suddenly, he stopped. "No," he screamed. "No, no, no!"

Ida Mae and I stopped fencing to look at him. He held a Santa Claus suit high in the air, its pants dragging on the floor. Cooper didn't know Uncle Dick used that suit every Christmas at our family get-togethers. Cooper still believed, or did, until now.

"What's this doing here?" he asked, tears streaming down his cheeks. "Is Santa Claus dead?"

We heard more steps on the stairs, but I didn't wait. I ran to Cooper, knelt to hug him, wondering what I could say. He grabbed me and buried his head on my shoulder, sobbing as if he'd never stop.

"I want my mama," he said again and again. "I want my mama."

I looked up to see Aunt Bess staring at us. "Oh, I can't believe I forgot," she began. "I didn't remember that I had kept them all these years. I thought I'd thrown them away." Her voice shook as she spoke, and tears collected like raindrops in her eyes.

It took me a couple of seconds to understand that she wasn't talking about the Santa Claus suit. She was talking about the pirate costumes that Ida Mae and I were wearing.

Eleven

"Can we afford to call Mom?" I asked Aunt Bess. "I think Cooper needs to hear her voice. I know it's expensive but I'll pay you back as soon as I can."

"Don't you worry about paying for the call," Aunt Bess said, practically running to the telephone in the kitchen. "It's time we all found out how she's feeling. That baby must be about due."

Cooper stopped snuffling the second he heard Mom's voice. But he had to tell every little bit of the story about finding the Santa Claus suit so there wasn't much time for me to talk or for him to ask if Santa was real. Maybe Cooper didn't really want to know.

It took the rest of the afternoon to fix everything. We

had forgotten the brownies in the oven, and when Cooper started howling in the attic Aunt Bess had left one pair of Uncle Dick's shorts on the ironing board with the iron on them. So we started over, throwing out the burned brownies and shutting off the iron so we could scrape Uncle Dick's shorts off of it. But Aunt Bess said to look on the bright side, she now had a new dust rag.

Finally, things got back to normal and Ida Mae and I made another batch of brownies and Cooper licked the frosting pan. I kept waiting for Aunt Bess to say something about the costumes, but she only told us to take them off and put them back in the box.

"I'll talk to you later," she whispered to me when Ida Mae went to the bathroom. "It's family business."

"But they're only costumes," I answered.

"That's right, but she could say something, and before you know it her Grandma Dean would know."

I think she already does, I thought.

Then Uncle Dick came home with Grandanna. "Look who's coming to supper," he shouted, coming into the kitchen with her right behind him.

"Lordy, if it don't stop rainin' pretty soon, we won't have to go fishin' ever again," Grandanna said. "The river will run over its banks, and those fish will just float right into the kitchen." She picked up a fork and gave a test poke to the catfish sizzling in a pan on the stove.

Ida Mae and I unfurled Aunt Bess's freshly-ironed, red and blue plaid tablecloth and lowered it gently to the table before we set it with plates that had yellow daisies twined around the edges. I set out iced tea glasses, but there weren't enough for everyone so I put out a jelly glass for myself. Then Ida Mae poured the iced tea and didn't spill a drop.

"Are we getting too much rain for the moving job?" Aunt Bess asked Uncle Dick as she tossed the weed salad and added dressing.

"If it don't stop soon, we'll be in trouble," he said. I remembered his words up in the attic earlier this week. He didn't get paid until thirty days after he finished his work. No wonder he had his face tied up in a worried knot.

Finally, a bowl of boiled small, red potatoes, tossed with butter and dill, crusty rye bread, weed salad, and fresh peas from the garden joined a platter of fried catfish on the table. We sat down and Uncle Dick spoke to God about the food and the weather, reminding God that we could always use the food but we had more than our share of rain.

After we all said "Amen" Cooper added, "P.S. Please let me know before too long about Santa Claus, whether he is or he isn't. Nobody else seems to know. Double amen."

"What in tarnation was that all about?" Grandanna said, helping herself to the catfish.

Aunt Bess started to explain but Cooper had his own version. "I saw Ida Mae and Maggie all dressed up like pirates, and then I looked for a costume for me and found the Santa Claus suit and it gave me the worries and I started to cry because I thought . . . "

Grandanna put her fork down on her plate with a clatter. "Where's your thinkin', Bess? How come you left those costumes around for her to find?" She gave me a glance laced with meaning.

"They're just costumes, aren't they?" I repeated what I'd asked earlier. I looked at Ida Mae to see if she could make sense of all this. But she was eating as if she was going to be graded on her efforts, chewing with total concentration. Grandanna noticed too.

"Don't eat too fast now," she said. "You don't want to choke on a fishbone."

Ida Mae stopped chewing. "Is there a chance I could?"

"Of course," Grandanna said. "Once, when Lolly was a little girl, she near about choked to death. Thought we'd have to take her all the way to Peoria to get a doctor to pull that durn thing out of her throat."

"What happened?" Cooper's eyes grew as round as the

peas on his plate as he put his fork down beside his uneaten catfish.

"Nothin'." Grandanna helped herself to more fish. "We turned her upside down and it come loose."

"It sure is dangerous eating at your house," Ida Mae said, looking at me. "First, poison mushrooms, now pointy fish bones." Before long, however, she began to eat again, as though she had measured the odds and found them in her favor.

"No one has answered my question," I said in the silence that followed. "I said what's so important about those pirate costumes? It's not as if somebody died in them."

Aunt Bess and Grandanna made a funny sound, not funny to laugh at, but totally unlike anything I'd heard before. They sat kind of paralyzed, forks half-way to their mouths, while Uncle Dick stared out the window. The quiet rumbled like thunder.

"Did something just happen?" Cooper asked.

"I didn't really mean it." Ida Mae began. "I mean, that stuff about eating poison and bones and such. It's all good food and better than I've ever had in my life. Honest."

Still, no one moved.

"I mean it," she tried again.

"It's not you, Ida Mae," I told her. "I just said something, and it must have meant more to someone else than it did to me. I don't know why everything is such a big secret. Somebody knows though and has to tell me. You all keep putting me off, pushing me away, but I'm almost grown up now, and so . . . so, you've got to tell me. What's going on?" I took a deep breath. "What's my name?"

"I meant to throw those costumes away," Aunt Bess began. "I really did mean to, Mama," she said, looking at Grandanna. "Or maybe, I told myself that I did. I don't know why I didn't. Maybe I wanted it all to come out. Maybe . . . "

"Bess, you can talk about this some other time." Uncle Dick reached over and held her hands. "It can be later, when you're more comfortable."

"No," she said. "Like Maggie said, it's time she knew. That is, if you don't mind, Dick. Will you be all right if I talk about it?"

"Sure, honey. You know I love you, no matter what." Uncle Dick kissed her hand and for a second, I knew there wasn't anyone in the room for him but Aunt Bess.

I looked at each person around the table as I waited for Aunt Bess to begin. Uncle Dick held on tightly to Aunt Bess's hands, Cooper pretended that he was paying attention, but he was really pushing all of his weed salad under a piece of catfish on his plate. And Ida Mae had stopped eating and stared at me with great big questions in her eyes. She wanted answers too, if I was going to be her best friend.

Then I looked at Grandanna. Oh, no. "Grandanna, are you all right?" I stood up and knocked over my chair.

Her face had turned blotchy red, and she seemed to be choking. "Grandanna." Now I yelled at her and grabbed her arm just as she started to slump over her plate.

Uncle Dick jumped up and pulled her up by the shoulders before she fell over completely. "Anna," he shouted. "Anna, can you hear me?"

She made a funny gargling sound as if words had stuck in her throat.

"Mama, what's wrong?" Now Aunt Bess held onto Grandanna's other shoulder. "Tell me where you hurt. Can you get your breath?" Her voice grew shaky.

"It's them fish bones," Ida Mae said suddenly. "One got her."

Grandanna shook her head. She tried to say something.

"Pills," I yelled. "That's what she's saying. She needs those pills old Doc Grogan gave her."

"How do you know about any pills?" Aunt Bess looked surprised first, then startled, then suspicious.

"I just know. Grandanna, where are your pills?" I didn't have time to be polite.

"I'll call Doc Grogan," Ida Mae said quickly. "I had to do that for my grandma." She ran to the telephone and began to dial.

"In my hair," Grandanna mumbled. "I keep the pills in my hair so I'll have 'em handy."

"Your hair?" Aunt Bess shook her head. "It's not possible."

I pushed Aunt Bess aside and began to feel through Grandanna's thick, curly hair. A pill fell out onto the table, then another and another. I grabbed one and shoved it in her mouth. Ida Mae held a glass half-filled with ice tea so Grandanna could take a drink and get the pill down. After a minute she seemed to breathe easier.

"Just a little spell," she whispered. "I'll be all right."

Uncle Dick pulled up a chair next to Grandanna. "Sit down here, Bess," he said.

She sat down and let Grandanna slump against her. "Doc Grogan's on his way," she said, cradling her mother in her arms. "Meantime, we'll just sit here nice and quiet. I love you, Mama."

"Promise me one thing, Bess." Grandanna spoke softly. "That you tell Maggie everything. You got to promise or I won't rest easy."

I looked around, suddenly remembering Cooper. He hadn't moved, but now, when he saw me looking at him, his mouth began to quiver and tears overflowed his eyes.

"Is she going to die?" he whispered. "Is Grandanna going to die?"

Twelve

Old Doc Grogan tried to get Grandanna to go to the hospital in Galesburg, but she put up such a big fuss, he finally let Aunt Bess take her home and stay with her until Grandanna felt better.

After old Doc Grogan left, Cooper and I hugged each other for a long time. I could feel his little bones shaking from seeing Grandanna like that. I was scared plenty too, but tried hard not to show it, at least on the outside. Worrying about Mom and now Grandanna made my eleven-year-old head pound. If the grownups are in charge of the world, why don't they do something about making it easier on everybody, especially kids? We aren't supposed to start worrying until we come of worrying age.

I forgot Ida Mae was there until I turned around and saw her tucked away in a corner by the stove.

"Do you need a hug too?" Cooper asked her, holding me so tight across the middle I felt like a sack of flour ready to burst from all my seams.

"Think so," she said, and raced over to the middle of the room and threw her arms around both of us.

After a while we stopped hugging and broke apart to wipe our eyes. I looked up to see Uncle Dick, standing in the doorway to the dining room, looking at us as if we might have something contagious that he didn't want. It wasn't like him to act this way.

He had his hands in his pockets, clinking his spare change together. "Grandanna's gonna be okay," he said softly. "Only, she's already done a lot of living, so . . . so . . . " His voice tailed off and he looked away from us.

"Should we call my mom?" I asked.

Uncle Dick looked at me suddenly, as if it was a brand new thought. Maybe it was. "You mean Edie?"

"Yes, Uncle Dick." What was his problem?

"Of course," he said quickly. "I wasn't thinking. We'll ask Bess first though."

But Aunt Bess said not to disturb Mom any more because of her delicate condition. Grandanna's spell had been all the commotion Mom could take just now.

The next day Cooper and I decided to try cooking noontime dinner. We didn't call Aunt Bess with a lot of silly questions either, like how do you get spare ribs out of a pan that refuses to give them up. We finally threw everything away even though Uncle Dick said that might have been Aunt Bess's favorite pan. I don't think she'd have thought so anymore. The following morning we had to air out the house after we forgot the eggs boiling on the stove until they blew up and made yellow polka dots on the ceiling.

On the third day Aunt Bess called us. "I'm coming home," she said, sounding as tired as I've ever heard her. "Lolly just came back from Galesburg, and she'll take over now."

Uncle Dick picked her up and brought her home. She said she was too tired to walk two blocks, then she went right upstairs to take an hour's nap.

"Let's fix supper for Aunt Bess," Cooper suggested.

"Good idea," Uncle Dick said, acting like he was somewhere else. A minute later he said, "Got to go out to the house that I'm gonna move, and then run downtown. Try not to make any noise while you're cooking so's Bess can get some rest." A minute later, his truck roared out of the driveway.

"What'll we fix?" I asked Cooper, knowing what he'd say.

"Banana cream pie," he answered the way he always answers Mom at home.

"I can do the banana part," I said.

"Okay." He sighed. "Guess we need Mom to do the rest." He paused before he asked, "Is she going to be all right?"

"You mean Mom?"

"Yeah, I mean Mom and all the other grownup ladies in the family. I mean Grandanna and Aunt Bess . . . "

"How about me?"

"Even you, Maggie." He grinned, then peeled a banana and ate it. So much for the pie.

"Everything's going to be just fine, you wait and see. One of these days we're going to have us a little brother or sister." Would it look a little bit like me? I wondered for the hundredth time.

I went to the pantry and found a can of baked beans. At least I could open that, and maybe there was something else in a can that I could open, too. I pushed some stuff around, but nothing sounded good. What were anchovy paste and hearts of palm anyways? Aunt Bess must have gone to that fancy store in Peoria and bought this stuff a long time ago, judging from the look of the cans. There was an old date on one of them. That was funny. She and Uncle Dick weren't even married then.

Cooper was rummaging through the refrigerator. "Hey, I found some ground-up meat," he said.

"Let me see." It turned out to be hamburger. "I wonder if I know how to make meat loaf," I said.

"I know one thing we're not going to have," Cooper said. "Not while I'm in charge."

"Let me guess." I hauled out ingredients for the meat loaf.

"Weed salad," Cooper shouted. "No weed salad tonight!"

I started mixing the meat loaf. "Make some cracker crumbs for me, will you?"

Before we finished, the kitchen and Cooper were covered in a fine dust of soda crackers. But we had enough for the meat loaf when I put it in the oven.

Aunt Bess came downstairs so soon that I thought we'd made too much noise. I started to show her what I was fixing for supper, but she stopped me.

"Let's take a walk," she said. Her voice sounded so strange it got me worrying that maybe there was more wrong with Grandanna than I knew about.

"Cooper, you can pick some nice weeds for salad," she called over her shoulder before we started out. I heard him say something from the living room but happily I couldn't make it out.

We walked a while before she spoke. Would she never begin?

Finally, she said, "Remember, when your grandma had her spell the other night and what she made me promise?"

"I guess I don't understand what she meant. I just hope she's feeling better."

"She's better all right. She hasn't left me alone for a second. Been talking morning, noon, and night about . . . about what it is I got to tell you."

My heart floated up into my throat and stopped there, waiting for something to happen. Maybe I was wrong. Maybe all this wasn't about me.

"It's about Mom, isn't it?" Finally, we were going to start talking. "She's got something else the matter, more than the baby . . . "

"No, Maggie. It's not that."

"I know." I grabbed at any thought that came into my head. "I had a twin, but Mom and Daddy had to give her away, or she died, or she was kidnapped . . . "

"Maggie," Aunt Bess gave me a little shake. "Listen to me."

"Then I'm adopted." I nodded my head. I could handle

that. "Lots of kids are adopted, and they're the lucky ones. So nobody's real in my family. Grandanna's not my real grandma . . . "

"Oh, but she is." Aunt Bess interrupted. "She's your real grandma, Aunt Lolly's your real aunt . . . "

"And you're my real Aunt Bess," I finished quickly. "Case closed. End of story. The end." Sudden tears splashed down my face and I felt I might drown in them if I heard one more word from her.

"You've got to hear the rest," Aunt Bess said softly.

"No, I don't have to." I put my hands over my ears.

"Yes, you do."

"But my mom, she's my real mom if you're my real Aunt Bess."

"No, I'm your mama." She said it so softly I hardly heard her at first.

"You mean, you feel like my mama." I corrected Aunt Bess. "You always say that when I come down to visit. That's because you're in charge, like a regular mama."

"Yes, I always say it, honey." Aunt Bess stopped to look at me. "Because it's true."

Suddenly I felt as if I was standing on the swinging bridge over the gully at Lake Bracken, leading to cousin Nancy's cabin. I felt like I did when the swing came up to meet me before I was ready to put my foot down. It made me dizzy and out of control, the way I felt now. In an instant I knew the message had changed, the day had changed, and my life had changed irrevocably, and I didn't want any part of it. I wanted it put back just the way it was. Put it back, somebody. Put it back.

"But I've got Mom." I heard my voice take on a kind of shrill, panicky sound. "I've got Mom. She's my mama. You're my pretend mama when I come to visit. That's all."

I turned and began to walk away.

Aunt Bess hurried after me. "Please, Maggie, let me explain." She grabbed my hand and pulled me towards her.

"No, I don't want you to. I mean, there's nothing to explain. I belong to Mom. My mom. Her name is Edie. She's your sister. I'm going home now. To Edie. Goodbye."

I shook free of her and ran blindly, not caring where I headed. At first, I heard Aunt Bess running behind me, then slowly, her steps faded. Then I realized I was going to Grandanna's, the way I did when I was little. In her soft, round lap, everything always seemed better, became better. But I was getting too big for laps now. Especially hers. And I couldn't escape forever. Soon now, I had to hear the truth and accept it. It was gaining on me, going to overcome me and crush me with its awful light. It was what I wanted, wasn't it?

As I approached Grandanna's, Ida Mae appeared on the sidewalk, waiting. "Your Aunt Bess is down at the corner," she said. "Are you trying to run away from her?"

"She says she's not my Aunt Bess," I yelled as if somehow all of this was Ida Mae's fault. "Can you beat that?"

"She ain't?" Ida Mae's spiderweb eyebrows drifted up to meet her hair. "Then who is she? And if she ain't her, then that makes you somebody else too. Come on and tell me then, just exactly who are you?"

Thirteen

I burst through the front door of Grandanna's house, then stopped by the faded, overstuffed chair in the living room. What if she was asleep? I might scare her.

"Is that you, Maggie?" Her voice came from the kitchen.

"Grandanna." I tried to pull myself together as I walked to the other room. "Am I bothering you?" My voice skittered all over the place.

"No, I've been expecting you." Grandanna cleared her throat. "We've been leading up to this conversation ever since you got here this summer. And it's time."

"Where's Aunt Lolly? I thought she was taking care of you now."

"Don't need nobody takin' care of me." Grandanna got

kind of uppity. "I sent her to the store to get some eggs so you and I could talk by ourselves. Don't take much to send her runnin' off to Roy. Now sit down, honey. I'm makin' silver tea."

I looked at the table, set with two cups and saucers, and milk and sugar. Then I sat and watched as she poured boiling water from the dented, copper teakettle to half-fill the flowered teacups.

"Silver tea?" My hand shook as I reached for milk and sugar, and poured generous amounts of both in my cup. "This must be a special time." Special, I thought. Just a little. Just a lot.

"Yes, silver tea. It's good for what ails you, child. Me, too." Grandanna added milk and sugar, stirred it in the hot water and took a sip. "Oh, my, that goes down real good."

"I always felt so grown up when you made it just for us." I took a sip. It was hot and sweet and soothing. Was it soothing enough to help me now?

"Your Aunt Bess and mama been wonderin' for a long time how to tell you about . . . about the mix-up in your life. I wanted you told before now so the tellin' might come before your questions did. But we waited too long."

"Grandanna, Aunt Bess said . . . " But I couldn't make the words come out. "How can it be true? I mean, if it's true . . ."

"Just listen, dear Maggie. Take it all in before you decide what to do with it." Grandanna cleared her voice and began. "Aunt Bess fell in love with a nice man, but his religion was not the same as ours."

"I didn't know that mattered."

"Didn't matter to us, but it did to his kin. Some folks are bothered by differences, but we mustn't judge 'em for it." Grandanna took another sip of tea before she continued.

"So Aunt Bess and this man ran away and got married, but they didn't tell anybody. Eventually they were gonna announce it when folks got used to seeing them together. So Bess lived here at home, and he lived in his furnished room. And they kept goin' out same as before. They loved dancin' at the Roof Garden and even went to the Halloween ball . . ."

"Dressed in pirate costumes?"

"That's right, dressed in pirate costumes. That night, on the way home, there was a terrible car accident and he was killed."

"Oh, no. Oh, no," I cried out. "Poor Aunt Bess."

"Yes, poor Bess, because she had just found out she was in the family way."

"What's that mean, Grandanna? That she was going to have a baby?"

"Yes, honey. She was going to have you."

"Me?" I stood up suddenly, knocking over my chair. "She really is my mom?" It was true then. Aunt Bess tried to tell me, but I wouldn't let her. Wouldn't believe her. I sat down with a thud. There was nowhere to go to get away from this truth that I wanted to hear, yet dreaded to know.

"Take a sip of your tea, honey," Grandanna said.

"But why did she, well, what I mean is, why didn't she act like my mom right from the first?" I felt so betrayed. I tried to gulp back tears but they wouldn't stop.

"She never tried to hide it, darlin' girl. That was never her intention. But when his family found out that Bess and George had been married, they blamed Bess for everything, even the accident. They acted like it was her fault. Of course that was their grief makin' them carry on so, but it still was a burden Bess didn't need to carry. So she went to live with Edie and Fred."

"My mom and dad, or at least they used to be."

"She stayed with them until you were born and then came back with you. But her husband's family demanded that she hand you over to be raised by them. Of course, she said no, although she said she'd give them chances to see you. Your other grandma was so distraught, nothing satisfied her. So one night, she sent somebody to come and take you. Kidnapped you right out of your bed. We had to call the police to get you back."

"I don't remember that."

"You were brand-new, honey. Bess was so afraid for your safety that she took you back to Edie and Fred. Bess needed to work though, so she came home to her courthouse job. She didn't intend to leave you in Chicago, but your other grandma wouldn't leave Bess alone. Once, when Edie and Fred brought you down for a visit, your other grandma brought you presents and then tried to take you away with her."

"The lady in the big black hat."

"That's who it was. I don't mean to speak ill of her, but she said she'd never give you up. Never. She'd lost her only child and wanted you to fill his place."

I slumped back in my chair. This was almost too much to grab hold of and I didn't know if I could handle much more. The tears kept on coming as if they would never stop.

"Shall I go on?" Grandanna asked, leaning forward to look deep into my eyes. "There's not much more."

"Okay," I whispered. "Okay."

"You stayed with Edie and Fred after that, for your own protection. A few years later, your other grandma passed away, and Bess felt safe in letting you come down here for visits. But you seemed so happy as Edie and Fred's little girl that she let you live on with them. You didn't know you weren't really theirs, and when you started to talk, you called them Mommy and Daddy. It was a real sacrifice for her to do that, believe you me, but she wanted you to be happy more than anything else in the world. Then she met Uncle Dick and you know the rest."

Finally, the tears slowed down until I could see into the teacup. The silver tea had grown cold just like my insides, as if my feelings and thoughts had frozen into a lump.

"There's one thing to be said about all this," Grandanna concluded. "You're still stuck with me for a grandma."

"The only good thing." My voice sounded kind of brittle, hard, ready to break.

"Now, Maggie, it seems like we got a little more to talk about. I know this news is a shock and it will take time to get used to it. But it's up to you what you decide to do with it. This is the morning time of your life, Maggie."

"Morning time?"

"You've got most of your life ahead of you. You can spend it feeling mad and upset and making others around you feel upset as well."

"Well, I am upset, Grandanna," I shouted. "Plenty."

Grandanna waited for a second, then she went on. "They loved you, Maggie. All those people who wanted you in their lives loved you. Try to remember that and then pass it along. The love part, I mean."

I stood up. "Grandanna, I need to think about things. Maybe a walk will help."

"I understand," she said.

It was only when I leaned over to kiss her cheek, that I felt my tears touch hers.

The screen door squeaked behind me as I hurried outside. Ida Mae was waiting under the cherry tree in the backyard. Bees hummed around her as they searched out openings in the remaining fruit on the tree.

"What are you gonna do?" she asked. "Are you gonna stay here or go back home?"

"Have you been listening all this time?"

"Screen doors don't keep no secrets," she said.

I leaned against the tree with her. "What would you do?"

"Don't know." She shrugged. "Just wish I had a choice like that to make."

Then she looked me square in the face with her pale blue eyes. "Some folks have all the luck."

Fourteen

Aunt Bess came while I was talking to Ida Mae and said she could spend the night if she wanted. She wanted all right and came right over as soon as she told her grandma and packed her pajamas and toothbrush in a grocery bag.

I didn't pay much attention to her though. I went to bed early and left Ida Mae playing Monopoly with everyone else. While I waited for sleep to come, my mind wandered everywhere, from my earliest memories until now, this moment. Where had I been happiest? Where had I felt most loved? Where did I belong?

Morning came and jolted me back to what I'd learned yesterday. As the news re-surfaced, it felt like a bruise inside, instead of outside. Then I heard the muffled sounds of other voices and listened with a new awareness. Aunt Bess and Uncle Dick spoke softly from somewhere in the house. What did I call her now? Then I heard Cooper's voice and then Ida Mae's . . . Ida Mae! She'd stayed overnight. She'd been my first spender here, and I'd ignored her. Not that it mattered that much. She'd moved in the first day she walked in the backdoor, made a place for herself, felt acceptance and love, even recognizing it without having a lot of experience. Some people could do that.

There was a skittering noise at the door before it opened.

"She's awake," Cooper said, bouncing in to sit on the side of my bed. "Can I tell her?"

I sat up quickly. "Tell me what?"

Aunt Bess and Uncle Dick and Ida Mae followed him in.

"Sure." Uncle Dick ruffled Cooper's hair. "Go ahead."

"Daddy called," he began. "And guess what?" He paused to savor the moment. "We got ourselves a fine baby boy." Then he hugged me and deposited a maple syrup kiss on my cheek. "Oh, Maggie, isn't it fun to have a baby brother?"

I hugged him back. "I've always thought so. Now I've got two of them," I said and hugged him again. Then I met Aunt Bess's eyes for the first time since yesterday when she told me who I was. Finally, I could look at her again.

"There's more news," Ida Mae said. "Can I tell now?"

"It's your turn," Uncle Dick said.

"Uncle Dick's going to move the house today, and we get to ride in the truck with him."

"And then there's one more surprise when we move the house to its new home," Cooper said. "But he won't tell us what it is."

"Then it won't be a surprise," Aunt Bess said.

"Come on," Uncle Dick said. "Hop out of bed, Maggie. I'm going over to the house now, and I'll meet you all there in an hour."

For once Aunt Bess didn't have to tell us to hurry and get in Grandanna's old Chevrolet. She'd given it to Aunt Bess a few years back when neighbors began to complain about Grandanna driving over their front lawns. She said it was downright unneighborly of them but I think she was glad to get rid of that old car.

The house was ready to go when we arrived, and so was Uncle Dick. The house had been sitting on jacks for some time before Uncle Dick and his handy man, Scurry Biggs, chained it to the big dollies for the trip behind the truck. Now it was ready to roll.

"Climb aboard," Uncle Dick hollered to us, opening the truck door. We scrambled out of the Chevy and inside the truck.

"I'll see you later," Aunt Bess called and drove away.

Uncle Dick hopped in beside us. "Ready?" He asked.

"Ready, set, go!" Cooper shouted.

Uncle Dick looked in the rear view mirror and gave a thumbs up to Scurry Biggs who jumped on the front porch of the house to watch that the chains on the dollies didn't break. Uncle Dick shifted gears and slowly, slowly, we began the journey. From a side road ahead, Officer Maloney, one half of the town's police force, pulled out to lead us in his black-and-white.

People stopped to watch us and waved as we drove by.

"I've never been a celebrity before," Ida Mae said, as she waved back.

We drove past the farm that had the Peonies for Sale sign in the front yard.

"Uncle Dick, do you think they've still got peonies left to sell?" Cooper asked.

"That sign's been there for years," he said, watching out of his sideview mirror. "I think they keep it there so's the birds have a place to rest."

We turned on to the paved road and Officer Maloney blocked traffic so we could proceed to the next turn-off. Folks got out of their cars and shouted as we drove by.

"Come on, Maggie," Ida Mae said. "Wave to our fans."

I sank back on the seat and laughed. What would I do without Ida Mae?

We turned in to the empty lot two hours later. Several other men were there to help Scurry race around unfastening the chains on the dollies. Then slowly, carefully, Uncle Dick backed the house onto the jacks that were waiting for it on the cleared off plot of ground.

Cars kept showing up, and I just supposed they were filled with curious people watching Uncle Dick. Then I realized that I knew most of the people arriving. Frank Cunningham and his band pulled up in two cars and began to set up their equipment. A few of our neighbors and some cousins were standing around, getting in Uncle Dick's way. Grandanna sat on the running board of the Chevie, cooling herself with a fan from Foley's Mortuary. The people who owned the house stood near it, caressing its old wood. I saw old Doc Grogan and Punch Hardaway carrying a couple of washtubs full of watermelon while their wives and Aunt Bess spread a tablecloth on a picnic table. Then I saw Preacher Johnson pile out of his car with his wife and six kids. What was going on?

I ran over to Aunt Bess. "Is there something I can do?" I grabbed some napkins before they blew away.

Ida Mae and Cooper hurried up. "Look," Cooper

shouted. "Look at Aunt Lolly!"

I turned and stared unbelieving. She was just getting out of a car, dressed in white, like a bride, with a veil and carrying a bouquet and everything. Then I saw Roy following her, looking like he'd swallowed a pickle, all dressed up in his church-brown suit. He even had a flower in his lapel.

"They're gonna get hitched!" Ida Mae shrieked.

"Gather round," Uncle Dick shouted, and he pointed to where the preacher stood by the just-moved house.

Folks came together, even some from off the street, as Frank and his band began to play "Here Comes the Bride." Then Aunt Lolly and Roy stood in front of Preacher Johnson, and he began to say those fancy words that make two people one. As soon as he said "I now pronounce you man and wife," a cheer went up and people began to throw flower petals.

Everybody moved to the table next and picked up plates and forks. Soon, the food had disappeared, including the wedding cake with Grandanna's boiled white frosting on it. Then the band began to play for dancing and I danced too, with Uncle Dick first and then Mr. Hardaway, before I turned to see Grandanna beckoning me from her perch on the running board of the Chevy.

I walked over to sit beside her. "I've been thinking about what you said," I began.

"Good girl." She patted my knee.

"But first, Grandanna, I've got one more question." I could hardly bring myself to ask.

"What is it, sweetheart?"

"What's my real name?"

Grandanna sighed and sighed. Then she sighed again. "You really want to know?"

Now it was my turn to hesitate. Finally, I said, "You're right, Grandanna. Why do I need another name to think about after all these years of getting used to the one I've got? Maggie Calhoun suits me just fine."

Aunt Bess walked up to stand in front of us. "Did you like Aunt Lolly's surprise?"

I stood up and we began to walk. "Yes," I said, and took her hand. "Mom needs me more than ever," I went on. "Now that we've got another little boy. And Cooper will need me too. Moving to a strange place like California will be hard on him at first."

"That's right," she said. Her dark brown eyes deepened with tears. "But you know I'll always be here when you come back to visit."

"I know." I paused, but finally had to say it. "I think I'll still call you Aunt Bess if you don't mind."

"I couldn't love you more whatever you call me."

"Me too. Me too." We hugged each other hard before she went back to dance with Uncle Dick.

I looked at the old house now in its new place. It looked as if it already belonged there.

Suddenly Ida Mae was standing beside me. "You're going, aren't you?" she asked quietly.

"Yes."

"But we'll always be best friends, promise?"

"I promise."

"Good. I've always wanted to be best friends with someone whose father was a masked man."

I stared at her. "What do you mean?"

"Remember that day in Grandanna's attic when I grabbed those pictures?" Ida Mae asked. "I didn't give all of them back. I kept this one so I could pretend this man was my daddy. But I guess I better give him back, now that he's yours."

I stared at the faded picture. A masked man in a pirate suit stared back. I didn't know him at all. "It's okay, Ida

Mae. You can keep him."

"You mean it?"

"I mean it. I've already got a daddy."

"Wow. This is my lucky day," she said.

"Mine, too," I replied. And it was. It really was.